喚醒你的英文語感！

Get a Feel for English !

喚醒你的英文語感！

Get a Feel for English !

外商・百大
英文口語
145 Essential Phrases for Business Conversation
勝經

作　者◎薛詠文

I'll back you up!

推薦序

　　會和您做生意的那些來自英語系國家的商務夥伴其實大部分都不笨。就算從您口中說出來的英文有點生疏，我們通常都還是可以理解您想表達的意思。同時，我們會自然而然地調整自己說話時的語法及字彙，來使我們說出口的英文變得較為淺顯易懂。人們只需要大約幾百個能互相理解意思的單字，就能收發訂單、交涉價格、安排運送，並完成各種基本的企業溝通機能。

　　但是在您開始用英文「進行企業溝通機能」前，您必須先要有可以進行這些機能的對象。您必須先和同事及商務夥伴建立起關係，也必須持續地維持並開發那些關係。能以較為細膩的表達方式自然地使用英文的能力就會在這種時刻發揮功能。以熟悉且真實的溝通方式建立起來的關係會更加牢固可靠；反之，冰冷且公式化的溝通方式則會對關係造成傷害。如果您在溝通的過程中時常必須將自己想說的話從中文翻譯成英文，或是背誦過時商用英文教科書上的例句，雖然對方也許能夠理解您想要表達的基本內容，但是其他不必要的訊息可能也同時被傳達出去了。不管您想表達的內容為何，您的語氣可能會不經意地顯得冰冷、不專業，或是造成尷尬的氣氛，同事及商業夥伴也會變得較不願意和您一起共事。

　　好消息是，英語系國家的人每天使用的商務用語其實並不比您目前在使用的英文難到哪裡去。您只需要稍微花點心思去瞭解它們之間的差異，並做些微的調整。本書包含了一系列由 Wendy 老師所精心整理的英文表達方式，讓您能輕鬆地開始學習自然的商務英文會話。Wendy 老師豐富的教學背景使她洞悉華語系的學生在學習英文時所須面對的各種挑戰。她多年與台灣數家國際企業的工作及合作關係也同樣深具重要性，這些經驗使她能以較為宏觀且實用的角度去看待商用英文，並清楚明白它們在真實商務場合中的正確使用方式。若您正在尋找能夠確實有效地提升商用英文能力的方法，本書絕對是您的不二選擇。

身為一名作者及商用英文學習書的編輯，我必須強調像 Wendy 老師這樣擁有實際商務背景及經歷的作者對於這類指導教材非常重要。有太多忙碌的專業人士都將時間花在學習一些根本僅存在於教科書內的英文上。那些英文不是一些無啥意義的陳腔濫調，就是一些誇張、空洞的時髦術語。在和現實中的人們互動時，上述兩種類型的英文都無法讓對方感受到絲毫誠意。若要對處於自然環境中的商用英文進行識別與分析，就必須要是一位具備獨特語文敏銳度的內行人才行。Wendy 老師就是那位內行人。而一旦您也體驗過這充滿溫暖、專業與真實感的自然商用英文，您一定也能成為一位內行人。

David Katz

（本文作者為貝塔語言出版資深英語主編）

Most of the English speakers you do business with are not especially stupid. Even if your English is a little rough around the edges, we usually have very little trouble understanding you. At the same time, we naturally adjust our syntax and word choices to make our own English easier to understand. With a shared vocabulary of just a few hundred words, we could place and receive orders, negotiate prices, arrange shipping, and perform any number of basic business functions.

But before you start "performing business functions" in English, you need someone to perform them with. You need to establish relationships with your colleagues and business partners, and you need to maintain and develop those relationships. This is when it pays to have a more nuanced command of natural English. Relationships are strengthened when communication is familiar and authentic, and they are damaged when communication is impersonal and formulaic. If you find yourself constantly translating what you want to say from Mandarin or parroting boilerplate sentences from an outdated business English textbook, the basic content of your message will probably be conveyed, but other unwanted signals will be sent along with it. The tone of your communication may come across as inadvertently cold, innocently unprofessional, or simply awkward, and colleagues and business partners will be less inclined to work with you—regardless of the content of your message.

The good news is that the phrases English speakers use every day to conduct business are not in any way more difficult than the ones you may currently be using. It takes just a moment of your attention to notice the difference and make the adjustment. And with the thoughtfully curated collection of natural English expressions in this book, Wendy Hsueh has done the heavy lifting for you. Her extensive teaching background has made her especially sensitive to the particular challenges faced by Mandarin speaking learners of English. Just as important are her many years of working for and with global companies in Taiwan, experience which has clearly given her a broad and valuable perspective on the ways English is used in real-world business settings. Those looking for an efficient and effective way to improve their business English could not ask for a better guide.

As a writer and editor of business English learning materials, the importance of choosing a guide with Wendy Hsueh's real-world business experience is something that I cannot emphasize enough. Too many busy professionals waste too much time learning the kinds of business English that exist almost exclusively in textbooks. That English is either watered-down jejune tripe or hyped-up buzzword-laden jargon. Both types come across as insincere when dealing with living, breathing people. To identify and analyze business English as it exists in its natural habitat requires an insider with a special sensitivity to language. That's Wendy Hsueh. And once you have experienced the real thing—business English that is warm, professional, and authentic—you'll be an insider too.

David Katz

前言

　　筆者七十歲的父親告訴筆者，五十年前他們學英文是直接照「發音」來翻譯的。比方說："This is a book." 就直接音譯為「這是一本『博克』。」──這種學英文的方式完全沒顧及字意，怎麼可能學得好？

　　三十年前筆者開始學英文時，所幸未經歷到「音譯學習法」，不過仍然停留在「任何句子都要中譯」的階段。課堂上閱讀課文時，老師要求每讀一句英文就停下來翻一句中文。長久下來，課文內容的「中文意思」是瞭解了，但是少了對「英文原文」的 comprehension（理解力）。而這種「中譯學習法」後來也衍生了不良的後果。

　　記得以前有位同學很喜歡將英文直接中譯，當人家說 "I'm sorry."（對不起）時，他要回答「沒關係」，就直接說成 "No relations."。這麼說是不會有人聽得懂的，還會貽笑大方。另外也曾聽過同學想說「黃牛票」，就直譯為 "yellow-cow tickets"。老外不懂中文，當然無法聯想 "yellow-cow tickets" 是什麼。（「黃牛票」的英文是 "scalped tickets"。）

　　在台灣，英語的「教」與「學」多半是為了應付考試，而花過多時間在記憶文法規則上。事實上，跟老外討論什麼是「受詞補語」，或「與現在事實相反的假設語法」如何應用等，他們並不瞭解也不在乎，反正就是口語上表達自己的意思嘛！有些道地的說法就是會這麼說，沒為什麼。就好像我們在講中文時，會在頭腦裡先想「哪個字是受詞？哪個字是動詞？」，然後再講出來嗎？完全不會吧！此處並不是說文法完全不重要，而是基本的句型、句子結構還是要能掌握，但最重要的是必須瞭解如何使用、在何種情境使用，而非死記文法規則。

　　某日筆者隨口說到「應該先把這些『鳥事』處理完」時，四歲的小女兒就問了：「為什麼是『鳥』？而不是『公雞』？」──這個問題問得好，但還真著實讓我愣住而無法回答呢！另外，筆者曾經有位加拿大籍的英文老師，每當遇到同學問他「為什麼會這樣講」時，他總是說：＂Don't ask me why. I don't know.＂（不要問我為什麼，我也不知道。）的確，語言是活的，其表達方式與使用者的文化、背景及說話習慣息息相關，嚴格說來並沒有所謂的規則，也沒辦法一一解釋。

　　台灣的英語學習者在口語表達時，或多或少都仍帶有一些「中文的影子」，或者乾脆直接翻譯中文字面上的意思，導致老外聽得一頭霧水。這種情況如果發生在日常生活當中，或許還無傷大雅；要是出現在商務溝通裡，萬一造成誤解，恐怕會對生意產生負面影響。

　　筆者在外商工作期間，曾有一位同事想表達「公司離我家很近」，而說出 ＂The company is very near my home.＂ 這樣的一句話。說實在的，硬要這麼講老外可能還是聽得懂，但就是充滿濃濃的中文味，既不道地也不自然。換作是老外表達的話，他們會說：＂My office is within walking distance from where I live.＂。其中片語 ＂within walking distance＂ 含有「很近、走路就可以到」的感覺，聽起來是不是就不一樣了呢？

本書分為十一個單元，包括：社交、簡報、談判、出差、電話、面試等商務情境，首先透過「實驗試寫」篩選出台灣英語學習者最容易脫口而出的「中式英文」，再依此討論並加以修正。讀者們可以從「老外這樣說」的句子發現，有時可能僅僅只是一個字的改變，無論語意、聽起來的感覺、道地感，甚至是商務溝通不可或缺的專業感，全都截然不同！此外，商務溝通裡會使用到的英文口語，當然絕非僅限本書所介紹的一百四十五句，而一句話也不會只有一種表達法，因此，在每個主題句之後更增加了「老外還會這樣說」，讓讀者們舉一反三，依照自己所遇到的情境靈活應用。

　　在與國際交流日益頻繁，許多公司陸續跟進將英文制定為內部官方語言後，台灣人學英文也有自覺了，除了不能按字面翻譯，死記文法規則也行不通；應該力求貼近老外的習慣用法與口語，才能讓他們精準地瞭解我們想表達的意思。由於國際商務溝通必須兼顧正式感與禮貌，真正會使用到的道地說法相較之下也許沒那麼多，希望各位讀者透過本書嚴選的句子及說明，感受到中英句構及表述思維的不同，今後在職場上若遇到類似情境時，能試著跳脫中文的思考框架，用「老外說的話」和老外溝通，如此一來，相信處理工作實務及同事之間的互動都會更加順暢！

Enjoy!

薛詠文

2013 年 9 月

CONTENTS

推薦序 2

前言 6

本書使用說明 15

Unit 1　社交寒暄 Socializing

1	初次見面。妳就是漢娜吧？我是傑克。	18
2	我來自台灣。	19
3	我的工作是軟體顧問。	20
4	這是我的名片，有需要的話請跟我聯絡。	21
5	今天天氣好熱啊！	22
6	妳穿這套洋裝真好看！	23
7	你多久出差一次？	24
8	若您有空，我可以帶您四處逛逛。	25
9	我對足球不是很有興趣，我比較喜歡棒球。	26
10	美國哪裡好玩？	27
11	你臉色不太好。你還好嗎？	28
12	明天要不要到我們家吃個晚餐？	29
13	謝謝您的邀約。但不好意思，我有事沒辦法參加。	30
14	我可以在這裡抽菸嗎？	31
15	我要走了，否則我會趕不上火車。	32

Unit 2　同事互動 Interacting with Colleagues

16	某些業務代表就只會踢皮球。	34
17	若我們再不硬起來的話，他們就會踩到我們頭上。	35
18	我明天行程非常緊湊。	36
19	慘了，我得整夜不睡趕報告了。	37

20	謝謝你給我這個機會。讓我好好地考慮一下。	38
21	路克就只會說些好聽的，所以你不要太相信他的話。	39
22	我真的想證明我上次的表現不是矇到的。	40
23	我們辦個派對來提振部門的士氣如何？	41
24	我們部門的預算又要被砍了，但這也是意料中的事。	42
25	我的錢包放在辦公室忘了帶，你可以幫我墊五十塊買杯咖啡嗎？	43
26	我要提早在午餐後就下班去看醫生。	44
27	我今晚沒辦法和你們出去。我要上大夜班。	45
28	亨利要開刀，所以接下來兩週會請病假。	46
29	麥奎爾先生已確認我們都會加薪百分之三。	47
30	我問老闆可不可以先預支薪水，但他拒絕了。	48

Unit 3　會議討論 Meetings

31	我們開始開會！	50
32	盧法斯先生今天休假，那由誰主持會議呢？	51
33	本會議將在三點前結束。	52
34	我們接著討論上市策略。	53
35	麥莉，這一點妳的看法如何？	54
36	不好意思，我可以插個話嗎？	55
37	對不起。可以再講一次嗎？我不太瞭解你的意思。	56
38	我們很快地問一遍看大家是否都同意。	57
39	你們應該會在本週五前收到會議紀錄。	58
40	讓我們先跳過這個問題。	59
41	我挺你！	60
42	你們提出的問題，我們一個個處理。	61
43	時間不夠，可以請你長話短說嗎？	62
44	下週我們可針對此提議做正式表決。	63
45	我們每兩週開一次會以檢討進度吧。	64

Unit 4　簡報演說 Presentations

46 我的簡報分四個議題來討論。 66

47 我準備了講義，現在發下去給大家。 67

48 若有任何疑問，歡迎隨時提出。 68

49 這張圖表大家看得懂嗎？ 69

50 這張投影片顯示了過去三年的業績變化。 70

51 從這些數字各位可看出，市場呈現大幅度的成長。 71

52 這帶出了下一個我想討論的重點。 72

53 我想行銷策略部分都討論到了。 73

54 在討論客戶意見調查結果之前，我們先休息十五分鐘。 74

55 現在歡迎大家針對我的簡報提問。 75

56 你可以針對定價再多做點解釋嗎？ 76

57 如果我的理解沒錯的話，你想知道這個專案的截止期限，對吧？ 77

58 這個問題恐怕超出今天簡報的範圍了。 78

59 簡報後我很樂意親自與你討論此事。 79

60 如果你需要進一步討論我剛才所講的內容，請寄 email 給我。 80

Unit 5　電話交談 Telephoning

61 您好，我是李珊妮。我要找丹佐・史密斯。 82

62 請稍候，我為您轉接。 83

63 請告訴他溫蒂打電話來過。 84

64 您有空的話，請回電給我。 85

65 您現在方便講話嗎？ 86

66 您講什麼我聽不清楚。可以說大聲一點嗎？ 87

67 太扯了！我已經在電話上等了快五分鐘了。 88

68 我現在在電話上。兩分鐘之後再回電給您可以嗎？ 89

69 不好意思，就先這樣。我要接另一通電話了。 90

70 我重複一次，以確認我記下的是正確資訊。 91

71 我打電話來是想約明天的開會時間。 92

72	我想打一通對方付費電話到休士頓。	93
73	我手機快沒電了。	94
74	我要進電梯了，收不到訊號。	95

Unit 6　面試問答 Interviews

75	這是我的榮幸。我一直期待和您談一談。	98
76	我在行銷管理方面有相當多的實戰經驗。	99
77	我可能有點完美主義，所以有時候我會過於注重細節。	100
78	我有強烈的意願和動力學習。	101
79	我希望在可以自我成長，同時也能做出長期貢獻的地方工作。	102
80	我在週末喜歡看電影、聽音樂，不過我也非常喜歡瑜珈。	103
81	我自認是有熱情、勤奮的員工，而且我很懂得如何與人相處。	104
82	除了理論之外，我也學到很多實務技巧。	105
83	我的強項之一是我適應新環境的能力很好。	106
84	過去兩年內，我成功地實行了有效的系統並產生出潛在客戶名單。	107
85	那是個很棒的經驗，因為我克服了種種困難。	108
86	這問題很有趣。給我點時間想想怎麼回答。	109
87	請問您何時會給我回覆？還是我應該主動跟您聯絡？	110

Unit 7　談判協商 Negotiations

88	讓我們先確認協商的順序。您認為如何？	112
89	既然我們今天的議程很緊湊，那我們是不是應該馬上開始討論？	113
90	如果貴公司能保證訂購五千組，我們願意提供八五折優惠。	114
91	我恐怕沒這個權限做那種決策。	115
92	我認為我們雙方都要做些讓步。	116
93	為了讓您放心，我們保證三天後會到貨。	117
94	暫停一下吧。說不定稍後可以發想出新點子。	118
95	我想合約中的所有細節都敲定了。	119
96	我們就見機行事吧！	120
97	我們需要試著跳脫框架來看此事。	121

| 98 | 我們看看有沒有折衷的辦法吧。 | 122 |
| 99 | 看來我們在交貨期這方面無法達成共識。 | 123 |

Unit 8　客戶應對 Interacting with Customers

100	您對我們的哪一項產品最有興趣？	126
101	就品質而言，我們的產品是業界第一。	127
102	如果我們訂購超過一千組，你可以給我們什麼樣的折扣？	128
103	我來電是想詢問一筆尚未結清的款項。	129
104	根據合約，款項必須在三十天內付清。	130
105	我不需要知道確切的數字。只要大概就好。	131
106	交貨作業時間也是我們必須考慮的因素。	132
107	運送時程視您的位置而定，但通常我們會在七個工作天內送達。	133
108	那些要求對我們來說太超過了。	134
109	我們的顧客滿意度在業界可說是最高的。	135

Unit 9　宴會用餐 Events

110	我今天不太想吃中式餐點耶！	138
111	你推薦什麼？	139
112	你們有素食嗎？	140
113	可以續杯嗎？	141
114	不好意思。我們已經等十五分鐘了，飲料還沒送來。	142
115	不好意思。這牛排太老了，我點的是三分熟。	143
116	我飽到吃不下甜點了。	144
117	你想喝點酒嗎？可以幫我拿一下酒單嗎？	145
118	要不要我幫你從自助餐台拿點吃的？	146
119	我可以跟你們一起聊天嗎？	147
120	你們家真溫馨。	148
121	這太棒了！但是你真的不需要破費買東西送我。	149
122	你能來真好！	150
123	謝謝您的盛情款待。	151

Unit 10　展覽諮詢 Trade Shows

124	明天就要參展了，可是印刷廠還沒把我們的文宣品印好！	154
125	設置一個專業的攤位有助於提升我們的形象。	155
126	您好。歡迎參觀。	156
127	歡迎來看看我們的樣品。這本是我們的最新產品型錄。	157
128	有興趣參加我們的比賽嗎？有機會贏得免費的 iPad 喔！	158
129	我很樂意為您示範產品操作。	159
130	您可以隨時打我們的免付費專線訂貨。	160
131	這款非常暢銷，而且目前正在促銷。	161
132	我們大多數的零件都是日本進口的。	162
133	產品的報價會依您的訂購數量有所不同。	163

Unit 11　出差旅遊 Traveling

134	你可以告訴我登機門在哪個方向嗎？	166
135	我可以在這裡兌現旅行支票嗎？	167
136	我們遇到幾個大亂流，全程大家都嚇壞了。	168
137	這筆款項我要刷卡。	169
138	我想要一張本市的地圖，謝謝。對了，你們有公車時刻表嗎？	170
139	真抱歉我們遲到了。附近的停車位有點難找。	171
140	到這兒來路好找嗎？	172
141	我的班機誤點，所以我錯過轉機了。	173
142	請問怎麼去火車站最快？	174
143	在我們去辦公室之前，您想吃點東西嗎？	175
144	歡迎來到台北辦公室。希望您喜歡這裡。	176
145	英國人非常地友善。我想馬上再去一次。	177

本書使用說明

我想表達

看到這句話，如果是你，你會怎麼用英文說？先不要往下閱讀，你也試著答答看吧！

說法比一比

「中式英文」和「老外這樣說」到底有什麼不同？透過對照，箇中差異一目瞭然。

大師提點

大多數的「中式英文」其實並沒有文法上的錯誤，但老外在日常生活中幾乎不會那麼說！「中式英文」囧在哪裡？如何微調會更道地？看這裡就知道！

實境對話

模擬示範老外自然說法，幫助理解使用情境。

老外還會這樣說

一個情境不只一種表達方式，提供更多類似或衍生的說法。

MP3 軌數

隨書附贈的 CD 收錄「實境對話」及「老外還會這樣說」，邊看邊聽邊跟讀，同步提升口說力和聽力！

---

131 我想表達 **這款非常暢銷，而且目前正在促銷。**

🔊 Track 132

中式英文 This one is hot goods, and now we're providing a promotion.
老外這樣說 This one is our best seller, and we're currently offering a discount on it.

🎓 大師提點

每家公司都有其賣得最好的產品，但若將「熱賣商品」直譯為 "hot goods" 那可就不好了，因為英文裡的 "hot goods" 是指「贓物」！此處使用 "best seller" 這個片語才不至於產生誤會。另外，雖然 "promotion" 是促銷的意思，但是在國外通常會直接表示「提供折扣」，因此只要說 "offer a discount" 即可。

👥 實境對話

A: This one is our best seller, and we're currently offering a discount on it.
B: That's good to know.
A：這是我們銷售最好的產品，本公司目前正針對它提供優惠。
B：那真是好消息。

📢 老外還會這樣說

❏ This is our top-of-the-line model.
還是本公司最頂級的型號。

❏ We offer a five-year warranty—by far the longest in the industry.
本公司提供五年保固，這是目前為止業界最長的保固年限。

🔍 關鍵字

top-of-the-line (同類商品中) 最頂級的　　warranty ['wɔrəntɪ] (n.) 保固

⚠ 職場成功 Tips

在展場中為吸引潛在客戶，強調優惠價格是方法之一，不過亦可突顯「老外還會這樣說」例句中提到的 "quality"（品質）、"warranty"（保固）等其他 unique selling proposition (USP)——產品賣點。

關鍵字

精選對話及加值例句中出現的重點字詞，讓學習更紮實。

職場成功 Tips

外商主管小叮嚀，提醒與老外工作的須注意事項，或補充相關實用句型。

Unit 1

★ ★ ★ ★ ★ ★ ★ ★ ★ ★ ★ ★ ★ ★ ★ ★ ★ ★

社交寒暄

Socializing

初次見面。妳就是漢娜吧？我是傑克。

🎵 Track 002

中式英文　Nice to meet you. Are you Hannah? My name is Jack.

老外這樣說　**I don't think we've met. You must be Hannah. I'm Jack.**

⚡ 大師提點

與人初次見面時，老外通常會以 "I don't think we've met." 當作開場白，傳達「我們之前應該沒見過面」的感覺，接著就互相自我介紹。另外，"My name is ..." 是我們初學英文時背的句型，但實際上美國人大多是講 "I'm ..."；假如名字有點長，為了方便對方記憶和增加親近感，則會這麼說："Hi, I'm Leonardo DiCaprio. You can just call me Leo."（嗨！我是李奧納多・狄卡皮歐，你可以直接叫我李奧。）

實境對話

A: I don't think we've met. You must be Hannah. I'm Jack.
B: Hi, yes. Nice to meet you, Jack.

　　A：我們好像沒見過面。妳一定是漢娜吧。我是傑克。
　　B：你好，我就是。很高興認識你，傑克。

老外還會這樣說

❏ Hi, I'm Jack. I just transferred here from the Singapore office.
　 你好，我是傑克。我剛從新加坡辦公室調過來。

❏ Hi, I don't remember seeing you at one of these events. I'm Jack.
　 你好，我不記得在其他活動上見過你。我叫傑克。

🔍 關鍵字

transfer [træns`fɜ] (v.) 轉調；轉接（電話）

⚠ 職場成功 Tips

通常在口頭問候的同時，也會簡單地握個手。而談話或握手時，眼神要看著對方，並面帶微笑。

中式英文 I am come from Taiwan.

老外這樣說 **I'm from Taiwan.**

💡 大師提點

這是一個台灣英語學習者最常犯的口語錯誤。許多人總是不由自主地講成 "I am come from Taiwan."，但是其中 be 動詞 "am" 後接動詞 "come"，根本不符合文法。正確應為 "I'm from Taiwan." 或 "I come from Taiwan."，兩者擇一即可，千萬不可混為一談。若要變化一下可以說："I was born and bred in Taiwan."（我是土生土長的台灣人。）

 實境對話

A: Are you from LA originally?
B: Actually, I'm from Taiwan.

　　A：你本來就是洛杉磯人嗎？
　　B：其實我來自台灣。

 老外還會這樣說

❏ **Where are you from?**
　你來自哪裡？

❏ **Are you from around here?**
　你來自這附近嗎？

❏ **Where did you grow up?**
　你在哪裡長大的？

❏ **I was born in Taichung, but I grew up in Taipei.**
　我在台中出生，但是在台北長大。

🔍 **關鍵字**

originally [əˋrɪdʒənlɪ] (*adv.*) 起初；原本
actually [ˋæktʃʊəlɪ] (*adv.*) 事實上；其實；真的
grow [gro] (*v.*) 成長；增加
grow up 長大；成熟

🔊 **Track 004**

| 中式英文 | My job is a software consultant.
| 老外這樣說 | **I work as a software consultant.**

💡 **大師提點**

在商務場合和別人互相認識,除了介紹姓名和打哪來的之外,更需要說明自己的工作或職業,以便今後有相關業務時可以聯絡。介紹工作所使用的句型通常是 "I work as a ..." 或是 "I'm a professional ...",其中加入自己的職位名稱即可。

 實境對話

A: So, what do you do?
B: I work as a software consultant.

A:那麼,您是做什麼的呢?
B:我的工作是軟體顧問。

 老外還會這樣說

❏ **I'm in sales.** ★

我是業務員。

★ "I'm a sales." 是錯誤說法!

❏ **I'm a software consultant.**

我是軟體顧問。

❏ **I work for a financial services company.**

我在一家金融服務公司工作。

🔍 **關鍵字**

software [ˋsɔft͵wɛr] (n.) 軟體
consultant [kənˋsʌltənt] (n.) 顧問
financial [faɪˋnænʃəl] (adj.) 金融的

4 我想表達 這是我的名片，有需要的話請跟我聯絡。

| 中式英文 | This is my business card. If you need me, please contact me. |

老外這樣說 **Here's my card. Give me a call if you have any questions.**

💡 大師提點

中英文的語句結構不同，並無法逐字翻譯，直譯往往就是造成囧英文的元兇。在跟客戶交換名片時，你也可以說：" If you'd like to call, here is my business card."，來加強「有需要服務的話就打電話給我」的語感。

實境對話

A: How can I get in touch with you?
B: Here's my card. Give me a call if you have any questions.

A：我要如何跟你聯絡？

B：這是我的名片。如果你有任何疑問，歡迎打電話給我。

老外還會這樣說

❏ **Let me give you my card. Let's stay in touch.**

我給你一張我的名片，我們保持聯絡。

❏ **Do you have a business card?**

你有名片嗎？（可以跟你要一張名片嗎？）

🔍 關鍵字

get in touch with 與……取得聯繫　　　　**stay in touch** 保持聯絡

⚠ 職場成功 Tips

拿到對方名片時看到姓名，比方說 "Jack Godbout"，若不確定發音，最好詢問一聲："How do you pronounce your last name?"（請問你的姓要怎麼唸？），以免唸錯而失禮。

🎵 **Track 006**

中式英文 I'm so hot today.

老外這樣說 **It's absolutely boiling out there.**

⚡ 大師提點

要表達「天氣熱」，若說 "I'm so hot."，外國人也能瞭解，但因為 "hot" 一字在俚語
用法亦有 "sexy/attractive"（火辣）之意，因此在商務場合為避免讓人會錯意，仍以
"It's hot today." 為較適宜的說法，其中 "It" 指的是 "weather"（天氣）。

曾有同學問我，用 "I'm hot." 表示「我覺得身體很熱。」有何不可？這是可以的！但
是這麼說通常會附帶說明原因。例如："I just finished a high-temperature yoga
class. I'm so hot."（我剛上完熱瑜伽課，所以我現在好熱。）

 實境對話

A: It's absolutely boiling out there, isn't it?
**B: No kidding. But the typhoon this weekend should cool things
off a bit.**

A：外面真是熱爆了，你不覺得嗎？
B：真的超熱！不過週末的颱風應該會讓天氣稍稍涼快些。

📢 老外還會這樣說

❑ **Hot enough for you?**
有夠熱的，對吧？

🔍 關鍵字

absolutely [ˈæbsəˌlutlɪ] (*adv.*) 絕對地；完全地
boiling [ˈbɔɪlɪŋ] (*adj.*) 沸騰的；酷熱的

⚠ 職場成功 Tips

商務友人來訪前，建議先針對其所來自的地區做些功課，例如瞭解一下當地的氣候狀
況，此舉有助於聊天時提及較適切的話題。筆者之前就有同事問來自德州的客戶：「冬
季是否會去滑雪？」；問來自伊利諾州的廠商：「平時是否會去海邊玩？」——像這樣
的問題恐怕會讓人搭不上話。註 德州不太下大雪；伊利諾州不靠海。

妳穿這套洋裝真好看！

🎵 **Track 007**

中式英文) Your dress is very beautiful.

老外這樣說) **That dress looks really good on you.**

⚡ 大師提點

要誇獎別人打扮出色，"Your dress is beautiful." 的重點似乎落在 "dress"（洋裝）本身，而忽略了穿的「人」才是主角。因此，改為 "That dress looks really good on you." 意思就較偏向「穿上這洋裝，妳真好看。」的感覺。請注意，若說成 "You look really good in that dress."（妳穿著那洋裝好美。）的話，恐怕會讓人想歪，在商務場合中稍嫌輕浮，故應避免。

實境對話

> **A: That dress looks really good on you.**
> **B: Oh, thanks! I like it too.**
>
> A：妳穿這套洋裝真好看！
> B：噢！謝謝。我也很喜歡。

老外還會這樣說

❏ **I really like that dress.**
　我很喜歡那件洋裝。

❏ **I really like your scarf. Where did you get it?**
　我好喜歡妳這條圍巾。在哪裡買的？

🔍 關鍵字

dress [drɛs] (*n.*) 洋裝
scarf [skɑrf] (*n.*) 圍巾

⚠ 職場成功 Tips

雖然適時讚美是好意，但是在商場上，讚美別人時應點到為止。重點還是要放在業務的議題上，以免讓人會錯意，導致影響生意洽談。

7 我想表達 你多久出差一次？

🔘 Track 008

中式英文　How many times do you take a business trip?
老外這樣說　**How often do you travel on business?**

 大師提點

"How many times ..." 是「有幾次」的意思，若要傳達「多常／頻率」之意，則須使用 "How often ..." 這個句型。另外，「出差」也有幾個固定的說法，例如："travel on business"、"go to [place] on business" 或 "take a business trip" 等。

 實境對話

A: I just arrived from Hong Kong yesterday, and I'm flying to Seoul on Friday.
B: Wow. How often do you travel on business?

　A：我昨天才剛從香港回來，週五還要飛去首爾。
　B：哇！你多久出差一次呀？

🔊 **老外還會這樣說**

❏ **How often do you come to Taiwan?**
　你多久來台灣一次？

❏ **Do you spend a lot of time traveling?**
　你花很多時間出差嗎？

❏ **It must be hard to spend so much time on the road.**
　長時間舟車勞頓一定很累吧？

❏ **It must be tough to have to spend so much time traveling.**
　得花這麼多時間出差在外，一定很累吧。

🔍 **關鍵字**

arrive [əˋraɪv] (v.) 抵達；到來
arrive from 從某處返回
on the road 在路上；途中
tough [tʌf] (adj.) 難以應付的；剛強的

8 我想表達 若您有空，我可以帶您四處逛逛。

🎧 Track 009

中式英文　If you're free, I can bring you to see other places.

老外這樣說 **If you have some free time, I'd be happy to show you around.**

💡 大師提點

中文裡的「帶 [某人] 去 [某處]」，經常被誤翻為 "bring [someone] to ..."，但英文是使用 "take" 這個動詞來代表「帶去 / 帶領」之意。另外，「帶人四處走走 / 導覽」用 "show [someone] around" 是最自然的口語說法。

實境對話

A: I've had so many meetings this week that I haven't seen much of the city yet.

B: If you have some free time, I'd be happy to show you around.

A：我這禮拜開了好幾個會，都沒機會好好參觀一下這個城市。

B：如果您有空，我很樂意帶您四處逛逛。

老外還會這樣說

❑ **Have you been to the National Palace Museum yet?**

你去參觀過故宮博物院了嗎？

❑ **Would you be interested in seeing a little bit more of the city?**

你有沒有興趣走走多看看這座城市？

❑ **Are you interested in doing a little sightseeing, or do you just want to take it easy?**

你想四處走走、逛逛嗎？還是你想多休息一下？

🔍 關鍵字

sightseeing [ˋsaɪtˏsiɪŋ] (n.) 觀光；遊覽

take it easy 放輕鬆；別著急

9 我想表達 我對足球不是很有興趣，我比較喜歡棒球。

中式英文 I'm not very interested in football. I love baseball more.

老外這樣說 **I'm not much of a football fan. I'm more into baseball.**

 大師提點

若要談論自己喜歡或不喜歡的活動，僅用 "I like ..." 或 "I don't like ..." 來表達則稍嫌單調而無法拓展話題，不妨嘗試改用其他句型。例如，「喜歡」："I'm a big fan of ..."、"I'm totally crazy about ..." 或者是 "There's nothing I like more than ..." 等；「不喜歡」："I don't care much for ..." 或 "I can't stand ..." 等。

 實境對話

A: Some of us are going to a bar to watch the Manchester United match. Want to come?

B: I'm not much of a football fan. I'm more into baseball.

A：我們幾個人要去酒吧看曼聯足球比賽，要不要一起來？

B：我對足球不是很有興趣，我比較喜歡棒球。

📢 **老外還會這樣說**

❏ **Are you following the NBA playoffs?**

你有在看 NBA 籃球季後賽嗎？

❏ **I don't really follow sports, but I love to swim.**

我並不常看球賽，不過我很喜歡游泳。

🔍 **關鍵字**

match [mætʃ] (n.) 比賽；配合；適合   **playoff** [ˋpleˏɔf] (n.) 最後決賽階段；季後賽

⚠ **職場成功 Tips**

外國人非常喜歡討論球賽，例如英國人鍾愛足球、美國人喜歡橄欖球和籃球，日本人則熱衷於棒球等。因此，不妨事先打聽一下，來訪的商務友人其國家流行什麼球類運動，先準備些話題才聊得開。

美國哪裡好玩？

🎧 Track 011

中式英文 What places are good to play in the America?
老外這樣說 **What should I see while I'm in the US?**

 大師提點

自從電視上某個飲料廣告裡一名演員說："It's good to drink?" 之後，同學們就套用到口語中，像是 "It's good to play." 或 "It's good to read." 等。此說法嚴格說來並非錯誤，只不過，實際上老外並不會那麼說！

 實境對話

A: What should I see while I'm in the US?
B: It depends on what you like, but I think you'd have a great time in New York.
A：我到美國時應該去哪逛逛？
B：那要看你喜歡什麼，但是我想你去紐約應該可以玩得很盡興。

📣 **老外還會這樣說**

❏ **What do people in Utah do for fun?**
住在猶他州的人都做些什麼休閒活動？

❏ **Is there anything interesting to do in Iowa City?**
愛荷華市有什麼好玩的活動嗎？

❏ **I've never been to Dallas before. What's it like?**
我沒去過達拉斯。那是個怎麼樣的地方？

❏ **I've always wanted to visit Dublin. What's fun to do there?**
我一直想去都柏林看看。那裡有什麼好玩的？

🔍 **關鍵字**

depend on 視（某事物）而定
for fun 為了好玩；娛樂性質

你臉色不太好。你還好嗎？

🎵 **Track 012**

中式英文 Your face color is bad. Do you feel fine?

老外這樣說 **You look a little pale. Are you all right?**

 大師提點

臉色蒼白、臉色不佳可以使用 "pale" 這個字來表達；反之，可用 "You look wonderful."，或 "You look fantastic." 等傳達「你看起來氣色很好。」之意。

 實境對話

A: **You look a little pale. Are you all right?**
B: **I'm OK, thanks. It's just a cold, I think.**

A：你臉色不太好。你還好嗎？
B：我還好，謝謝。可能只是感冒。

👤📢 **老外還會這樣說**

❑ **Would you like to see a doctor?**
你想去看醫生嗎？

❑ **I'd be happy to get some medicine for you.**
我很樂意去幫你拿些藥。

❑ **Let me take you to see a doctor just in case.**
以防萬一，我現在就帶你去看醫生。

❑ **Why don't I take you back to your hotel now?**
我現在就送你回飯店吧。

🔍 **關鍵字**

pale [pel] (*adj.*) 蒼白的
cold [kold] (*n.*) 感冒
medicine [ˋmɛdəsn] （內服）藥
just in case 以防萬一

12 我想表達 明天要不要到我們家吃個晚餐？

🎧 Track 013

中式英文 Would you like to come to our home to have a dinner with us tomorrow?

老外這樣說 **We were wondering if you'd like to come to our place for dinner tomorrow.**

💡 大師提點

一開始就用 "Would you like to …?" 會顯得太直接，若改用 "We were wondering if you'd like to …" 聽起來就較客氣。比方說："We were wondering if you'd like to join us for dinner."，或 "We were wondering if you'd like to come to the party?" 等。

實境對話

A: **We were wondering if you'd like to come to our place for dinner tomorrow.**

B: **That sounds wonderful. Thank you. I'd love to.**

A：我們想邀請你明天到我們家吃晚餐。

B：聽起來很棒，謝謝。我很樂意去。

老外還會這樣說

❏ A few friends are getting together at my place after work on Friday. Would you like to come?

週五下班後幾個朋友會到我家聚聚。你想要一起來嗎？

❏ I wish I could, but I can't tomorrow. Maybe some other time?

真希望我可以，但是明天我不行。或許改天吧。

🔍 關鍵字

wonder [`wʌndə] (v.) 想知道　　　　**get together** 聚會

⚠️ 職場成功 Tips

商務友人邀約用餐或活動的機會很多。若要出席的話，最好詢問一下活動細節，比方說，是正式或非正式活動（formal/informal）、有無服裝規定（dress code）等，以免出現大家都穿西裝，只有你穿 T 恤出席的窘境。

謝謝您的邀約。但不好意思，我有事沒辦法參加。

🎵 Track 014

中式英文　Thank you for your invitation. But I'm sorry that I have a plan so I can't go.

老外這樣說　**Thank you for your offer. But I'm sorry, I won't be able to join you.**

💡 大師提點

受人邀約如因有事而必須婉謝的話，除了上述例句外，也可套用以下這個基本句型："I'd love to, but ..."。先表達參與的意願，再以 "but" 帶出轉折之語感，最後再說明原因就更加不會失禮。例如："I'd love to, but I already have plans."，或 "I'm afraid I can't make it. I'm going to Japan over the weekend." 等。

實境對話

A: There's a big karaoke party after work on Friday. Would you like to join us?

B: Well, thank you for your offer. But I'm sorry, I won't be able to join you.

A：週五下班後我們有個大型卡拉 OK 歡唱派對。你要不要一起來？

B：嗯，謝謝你的邀請。但是很抱歉，我沒辦法參加。

老外還會這樣說

❏ **I wish I could, but I really have to catch up on my rest.**
真希望我可以，但是我真的需要補眠休息一下。

❏ **That sounds like so much fun. I wish I could, but maybe next time.**
聽起來真的很好玩。真希望我能夠參加，不過還是下次好了。

🔍 關鍵字

karaoke [ˌkɑrɑˋoke] (n.) 卡拉 OK；KTV
offer [ˋɔfɚ] (n.) 提議；提供；開價；（工作）機會
catch up on 彌補；趕完
catch up on one's rest 補眠

14 我想表達　我可以在這裡抽菸嗎？

🎵 Track 015

中式英文　May I smoke here?

老外這樣說　**Is it all right if I smoke here?**

🔋 大師提點

詢問他人「是否可以…… [做某事] ？」時，較道地的說法有以下幾種："Do you think it's all right …?"、"Is it OK if I …?"、"Do you mind if I …?"，或者是 "Do you think I could …?" 等都很自然。

實境對話

A: Is it all right if I smoke here?

B: I'd rather you didn't.

　A：我可以在這抽菸嗎？

　B：最好是不要。

老外還會這樣說

❑ **Do you mind if I open the window?**

　- Not at all. Go ahead.

　- Actually, I do.

你介意我開窗戶嗎？

- 一點也不，請便。

- 事實上，我介意。(請不要開窗戶)

❑ **Do you mind if I step outside to make a quick phone call?**

你不介意我出去外面打個電話吧？

❑ **Would it be OK if I just opened the window a little more?**

我把窗戶稍微開大一點，可以嗎？

🔍 關鍵字

smoke [smok] (v.) 抽菸

not at all 一點也不

go ahead 進行；先走

31

15 我想表達　我要走了，否則我會趕不上火車。

中式英文　I'm going to leave, or I can't catch the train.

老外這樣說　**I'm afraid I have to go. I don't want to miss my train.**

💡 大師提點

與人道別時，若將「我要走了」，直接翻譯成 "I'm going to leave." 相當不禮貌。通常口語上會說 "I have to go."。之前有同學問過一個頗有趣的問題。他說美國朋友對他說 "I have to run." 時，他以為那朋友是要去跑步了，而事實上，"I've gotta run." 是另一句口語，指「該走了 / 趕時間」之意。

 實境對話

A: I'm afraid I have to go. I don't want to miss my train.
B: So soon? Well, we'll have to do this again sometime.

A：我得走了。我可不想錯過火車。
B：這麼快就要走了？那，我們只好下次再聚一聚了。

 老外還會這樣説

❑ **It's getting late.**
時候不早了。

❑ **I think I'd better be going now.**
我想我最好現在就出發。

❑ **I should think about heading back.**
我應該要準備回去了。

❑ **It's about time for me to think about heading back.**
該是我回去的時候了。

🔍 **關鍵字**

afraid [ə`fred] (*adj.*) 害怕的；擔心的；恐怕
miss [mɪs] (*v.*) 錯過；未得到；想念
head back 回去

Unit 2

★ ★ ★ ★ ★ ★ ★ ★ ★ ★ ★ ★ ★ ★ ★ ★ ★ ★ ★ ★

同事互動

Interacting with Colleagues

🎧 Track 017

中式英文 | Some sales people just try to let others take the responsibility.

老外這樣說 | **Some sales reps are always trying to pass the buck.**

💡 大師提點

"Pass the buck" 這個片語指 "blame other people or make them responsible for a problem"（為了一個問題指責他人或要他人負責），類似中文裡「踢皮球」的意思。順帶一提，前美國總統杜魯門在其白宮辦公桌上擺有 "The buck stops here." 的標語，用以傳達「不再踢皮球，責任我來扛」之意。

👨‍💼 實境對話

A: He said if the product were any good, he'd have no problem selling it. Can you believe it?

B: Don't worry. Those sales reps are always trying to pass the buck.

　A：他說如果這個產品真有賣點，他就不會賣不出去了。你相信嗎？

　B：別管他。那些業務總是在互踢皮球。

📢 老外還會這樣說

❏ **Those sales guys are always trying to pin the blame on somebody.**
那些業務總是想將過錯推到他人身上。

❏ **We all need to take responsibility for the problem.**
我們都應該對這問題負責。

🔍 關鍵字

reps = representatives 代表　　　　　**blame** [blem] (*n.*) 責備；指責

⚠ 商務成功 Tips

美商公司相當注重 "No excuses." 的精神，也就是說，遇到問題沒關係，只要有後續解決方案以尋求改進就好，最忌諱推拖找藉口。如果你一味推諉責任，美國老闆會跟你說："I don't want to hear any ands, ifs, or buts. Just do it now!"（我不要再聽任何「然後」、「如果」和「可是」了。現在做就對了！）

17 我想表達 ｜ 若我們再不硬起來的話，他們就會踩到我們頭上。

🔊 **Track 018**

中式英文｜ If we don't become hard, they will step on our heads.

老外這樣說｜ **If we don't show some backbone now, they're going to walk all over us.**

大師提點

商場上競爭激烈，若自己不硬起來展現出實力，就有可能被後進凌駕而上。在此所說的「硬起來」並不是真的 "hard" 的那種「硬」，因此以 "backbone" 代表「魄力／骨氣」較貼切。另外，「踩到某人頭上」就用 "walk over [someone]" 來表示即可。

實境對話

A: **We have to get serious. Our market share has shrunk five quarters in a row.**

B: **Yeah, if we don't show some backbone now, our competitors are going to walk all over us.**

A：我們必須嚴肅看待此事。我們的市占率已經連續五季下滑了。

B：是呀，如果我們現在不硬起來，我們的競爭對手就要踩到我們頭上了。

老外還會這樣說

❑ **If we don't get it together, they're going to kill us.**
如果我們不團結起來，他們就會把我們幹掉。

❑ **If we let them get away with this, I don't see how we'll ever recover.**
如果讓他們就這樣逃避掉，我看不出我們能怎麼回復到原來的狀況。

❑ **If our marketing strategies weren't so spineless, we could make a killing.**
要不是我們的行銷策略這麼弱，我們早就大賺一筆了。

關鍵字

market share 市占率
in a row 連續地；一個接一個地
recover [rɪˋkʌvɚ] (v.) 回復；恢復健康
strategy [ˋstrætədʒɪ] (n.) 策略；對策

quarter [ˋkwɔrtɚ] (n.) 一季；四分之一
get away with 僥倖逃脫；逃避懲罰
marketing [ˋmɑrkɪtɪŋ] (n.) 行銷
make a killing 大賺一筆；賺很多錢

我明天行程非常緊湊。

🎵 **Track 019**

中式英文　My schedule is very tight tomorrow.
老外這樣說　**I'm tied up all day tomorrow.**

💡 大師提點

上述的中式英文你是否也曾脫口而出？雖然老外勉強能理解你的意思，但對他們而言還是有點 "awkward"（囧）。要表示行程滿檔，道地的美語表達應是 "I'm tied up."，而其中 "tie up" 傳達了「緊緊著 / 困住」的感覺。

 ## 實境對話

A: Why don't we meet to discuss this tomorrow morning? Say, 9:30?
B: I'm tied up all day tomorrow.

A：我們何不約明天早上見個面討論此事？九點半如何？
B：我明天行程非常滿。

📢 老外還會這樣說

❏ **I have a full schedule tomorrow.**
我明天行程滿檔。

❏ **I've got a pretty busy day tomorrow.**
我明天一整天都會很忙。

❏ **My schedule is really busy tomorrow.**
我明天有好多事情要忙。

❏ **I won't have time tomorrow. How about Wednesday?**
我明天沒空。星期三可以嗎？

🔍 關鍵字

tied up 忙得不可開交的

⚠️ 商務成功 Tips

若同事想要約時間討論事情，除了表示行程很滿之外，最好也能主動提出其他方便的時間，以便對方行事。例如你可以這樣說："I'm busy this morning. How about 3:00 this afternoon?"（我今天上午很忙，下午三點好嗎？）

慘了，我得整夜不睡趕報告了。

🎧 Track 020

Unit
2

中式英文　Oh no! I need to stay awake all night to write this report.

老外這樣說　**Ugh! I'm going to have to pull an all-nighter to get this report done.**

 大師提點

說到「熬夜」，大家會自然想到 "stay up"，但是如果要傳達「通宵」的感覺，用 "pull an all-nighter" 這個片語比較傳神。另外，人在國外夜深了想吃宵夜時，若想問「這附近有開通宵的餐廳嗎？」，你可以說："Are there any all-night diners around here?"。

 實境對話

A: Ugh! I'm going to have to pull an all-nighter to get this report done.
B: Is there anything I can do to help?

　　A：慘了，我得做通宵才能將這報告趕完了。
　　B：有什麼我可以幫你的嗎？

📢 **老外還會這樣說**

❏ **It's going to take me all night to finish this report.**
我得花一整夜的時間才能趕完這份報告。

❏ **I'm going to be up late trying to finish this thing.**
要做完這件事，我整夜都不用睡了。

❏ **I'm not leaving here until I finish this thing.**
我得將這件事處理完才離開。

❏ **I'm not sure I'm going to be able to finish this by tomorrow.**
我不確定明天之前是否有辦法完成這項工作。

🔍 **關鍵字**

ugh [ʌg] (*int.*) 表示嫌惡、輕蔑、恐怖等的感嘆聲
pull an all-nighter 整晚熬夜
be up late 熬夜；晚睡

謝謝你給我這個機會。讓我好好地考慮一下。

🎧 Track 021

中式英文 ｜ Thank you for giving me the chance. Let me think about it well.

老外這樣說 ｜ **Thank you very much for the offer. Let me sleep on it.**

💡 大師提點

"Sleep on [something]" 指「經過徹夜沉澱後，將事情留到第二天再決策」，比起 "think about it" 更有「仔細考慮過再決定」的語感。順帶一提，"sleep" 這個基本單字，還可用在表達「自作自受」的慣用語中！你可以說 "You've made your bed, now sleep in it."，是不是非常貼切又有趣呢？

 實境對話

A: I wonder if you'd be interested in relocating to the Osaka office.
B: Wow. Thank you very much for the offer. Let me sleep on it.

A：我想知道你有沒有興趣調到大阪辦公室工作？
B：哇，謝謝你給我這個機會。我會好好地考慮一下。

 老外還會這樣説

❏ **That sounds like a wonderful opportunity. I'd love to. Thank you.**
聽起來真是個超棒的機會。我很樂意。謝謝。

❏ **That's a generous offer, but I'm afraid I have to decline.**
那是個絕佳的職缺，但恐怕我要婉謝你的好意了。

🔍 **關鍵字**

relocate [ri`loket] (*v.*) 調職；重新安置
sleep on 暫且擱置；留待隔天再決定
opportunity [ˌɑpə`tjunətɪ] (*n.*) 機會
generous [`dʒɛnərəs] (*adj.*) 慷慨的；大方的
decline [dɪ`klaɪn] (*v.*) 謝絕；婉拒；下滑

路克就只會說些好聽的，所以你不要太相信他的話。

中式英文　Luke's always saying good things, so you'd better not believe what he says totally.

老外這樣說　**Luke's a sweet talker, so you have to take what he says with a grain of salt.**

 大師提點

若要傳達「他說的話要打個折」這句話，不能直接使用 "discount" 這個字，而應以 "with a grain of salt" 這個片語來代表「有所保留、不全然相信」之意。另外，"sweet talker" 即中文裡「嘴巴很甜的人」。

 實境對話

A: He thinks I'm next in line for a promotion.
B: Well, Luke's a sweet talker, so you have to take what he says with a grain of salt.

A：他認為下一個升遷的人選就是我。
B：嗯，路克專挑好聽話講，所以你不要太相信他說的話。

老外還會這樣説

❑ **I wouldn't take what he says that seriously.**
我不會把他說的話全然當真。

❑ **I think he was just trying to flatter you.**
我認為他只是在講些奉承你的話罷了。

關鍵字

next in line for 下一個輪到
with a grain of salt 有所保留地

promotion [prə`moʃən] (n.) 升遷；促銷
flatter [`flætɚ] (v.) 諂媚；奉承

⚠ 商務成功 Tips

有幾分把握就說幾分話，在商場上更是如此。如果總是逢迎拍馬的話，就會被認為是一個 "brownnoser"（馬屁精）喔。

我真的想證明我上次的表現不是矇到的。

🎧 **Track 023**

中式英文　I really want to prove that my last performance was not a lucky thing.

老外這樣說　**I really want to show that last time wasn't a fluke.**

💡 大師提點

生活中真正在講的話該如何用英語表達，有時翻遍課本也無解。曾經有同學問我「矇到」的英文要怎麼講，透過上述例句就能發現，關鍵字就是 "fluke"，指「僥倖成功」之意。

 實境對話

A: Are you still working on that presentation? It's getting pretty late.
B: I really want to show that last time wasn't a fluke.

　　A：你還在準備那份簡報嗎？已經很晚了。
　　B：我真的想證明我上次的表現不是矇到的。

 老外還會這樣説

❏ **I'm really looking forward to showing everyone what I can do.**
我真的很期待將我的實力展現給大家看。

❏ **Good presentations take time. Last time wasn't an accident you know.**
要做好簡報得花不少時間。我上次的表現可不是僥倖。

❏ **There are a lot of people counting on me, so I want to make sure it goes well.**
很多人都指望我，所以我要確定事情順順利利。

🔍 **關鍵字**

work on 從事；做某事；工作
look forward to 期待

presentation [ˌprizɛn`teʃən] (n.) 簡報
count on 依賴；指望

我們辦個派對來提振部門的士氣如何？

中式英文　How about holding a party to cheer up the morale of our department?

老外這樣說　**What if we hold a party to increase department morale?**

💡 大師提點

"Cheer up" 指「使高興」，但是不能和 "morale"（士氣）連在一起使用來表達「提振士氣」，而應用 "increase morale" 來表示。另外，例句中所提到的 "the morale of our department" 也過於冗長，在口語中直接說 "department morale" 即可。

👓 實境對話

A: Well, we made the deadline, but everyone is exhausted.

B: What if we hold a party to increase department morale?

A：嗯，我們趕在期限內將工作完成了，但是大家也都累癱了。

B：那我們辦個派對來提振部門的士氣如何？

老外還會這樣說

❏ **Do you think throwing a party would help increase morale?**
你認為辦個派對能夠提振士氣嗎？

❏ **Why don't we all go out after work to celebrate?**
下班後我們大家去外面慶祝一番吧！

🔍 關鍵字

deadline [ˋdɛdˌlaɪn] (*n.*) 截止期限

make the deadline 趕在期限內完成某事

exhausted [ɪgˋzɔstɪd] (*adj.*) 精疲力竭的

hold [hold] (*v.*) 舉辦；等候；持續

morale [məˋræl] (*n.*) 士氣；鬥志

我們部門的預算又要被砍了，但這也是意料中的事。

🔊 **Track 025**

中式英文 ｜ Our department budget is cutting again, but that's not so surprising though.

老外這樣說 ｜ **The department budget is going to be cut again, but that's a par for the course.**

💡 大師提點

此句也是來自同學的提問。「意料中之事」的英文要怎麼講？大家第一時間腦中可能會浮現 "I knew that already." 或 "I'm not surprised." 等，這兩個說法雖然沒錯，但若是改用片語 "par for the course" 來表達則更加貼近老外平常的說話習慣。

實境對話

A: How was the meeting? Any big news?
B: The department budget is going to be cut again, but that's a par for the course.

A：會開得怎麼樣？有沒有什麼大事？
B：部門預算又要被砍了，但那也是意料中之事了。

老外還會這樣說

❑ **The department budget is going to be cut again, but we knew that was probably going to happen.**
部門預算又要被刪減了，但我們知道那也是遲早的事。

❑ **Our budget is going to be cut again, but what did you expect?**
我們的預算又要被砍了，要不然還會怎麼樣？

🔍 關鍵字

budget [ˋbʌdʒɪt] (*n.*) 預算
par for the course 意料中之事；難怪
probably [ˋprɑbəblɪ] (*adv.*) 大概；很可能
expect [ɪkˋspɛkt] (*v.*) 預期；預計；期待

我的錢包放在辦公室忘了帶，你可以幫我墊五十塊買杯咖啡嗎？

🎧 Track 026

中式英文 I forgot my purse in the office. Could you lend me NT$50 to buy a cup of coffee for me?

老外這樣說 **I left my purse in the office. Could you spot me NT$50 for a cup of coffee?**

Unit
2

💡 **大師提點**

國中時期大家都學過 "borrow"（借入）和 "lend"（借出）兩個字，但是中文「墊錢」裡的「墊」字在口語中要怎麼說，書本上卻沒有教。其實，老外們會用 "spot" 這個字來表示喔。比方說，買東西結帳時少了一百塊，你可以說： "Could you spot me a hundred please?"（你可以先幫我出一百塊嗎？）

 實境對話

A: **I left my purse in the office. Could you spot me NT$50 for a cup of coffee?**

B: **Sure, no problem.**

　A：我的錢包忘在辦公室了。你可以幫我墊五十塊買杯咖啡嗎？

　B：當然可以，沒問題。

 老外還會這樣說

❏ **I got the last one. I think it's your turn.**
　上次是我埋單。這次輪到你。

❏ **I forgot my wallet. Could you get this one?**
　我忘記帶皮夾了。這次就麻煩你了。

❏ **Could you get this? I'll pay you back when we get back.**
　你可以先埋單嗎？我回去再還你錢。

🔍 **關鍵字**

purse [pɜs] (n.) 女用錢包　　　　　　　**wallet** [ˋwɑlɪt] (n.) 皮夾；錢包

我要提早在午餐後就下班去看醫生。

🎧 **Track 027**

中式英文 I'll leave to go to see a doctor early after lunch.

老外這樣說 **I'm leaving right after lunch for a doctor's appointment.**

💡 大師提點

"I'm leaving + 時間 + for + 目的" 表示「某時間要離開去做某事」，而 "doctor's appointment" 則為「與醫生約診」。中式英文例句以 "go to see a doctor" 來表示「去看醫生」顯得有些不自然，通常口語說 "go to a doctor" 或 "see a doctor" 即可。另外，其後的 "early after lunch" 是「提早在午餐後」的直譯，既提到 "early" 又說 "after"，聽起來讓人感到迷惑。

🤓 實境對話

A: Could you finish this before you go home today?

B: Actually, I'm leaving right after lunch for a doctor's appointment.

A：你今天下班前能把這個完成嗎？

B：其實我今天吃完午餐就要下班去看醫生了。

📢 老外還會這樣說

❏ **I have a dental appointment scheduled for 2:30.**
我在兩點半預約了要去牙醫看診。

❏ **My kid is sick. I have to leave early today to pick him up from school.**
我的小孩生病了。我今天得早退去學校接他。

❏ **I'm not feeling well. I'm going to have to go home early.**
我感覺不太舒服。我今天得提早下班。

🔍 關鍵字

appointment [ə`pɔɪntmɪnt] (n.) 正式的約定（如商務會面、醫生約診等）
dental [`dɛntl̩] (adj.) 牙科的
pick up someone 接某人

我今晚沒辦法和你們出去。我要上大夜班。

Track 028

中式英文　I can't go out with you tonight because I have to work from 12 midnight to 8 a.m.

老外這樣說 **I can't go out with you guys tonight. I'm working the graveyard shift.**

 大師提點

公司輪班制裡的「大夜班」的英文怎麼說？通常半夜十二點到早上八點的工作時段，在英文以 "graveyard shift" 一詞來表達，因為這段時間通常是吸血鬼在墓地出沒的時候，他們也是「上大夜班」。這樣聯想是不是就變得很好記了呢！

實境對話

A: We're all going to meet up at the Roxy after work tonight. Want to come?

B: I can't go out with you guys tonight. I'm working the graveyard shift.

A：我們今晚下班後全都約好要去 Roxy。要不要一起來？

B：我今天晚上沒辦法和你們出去。我值大夜班。

 老外還會這樣說

❏ **Thanks, but I can't today. Maybe next time.**

謝啦，但我今天沒辦法。下次再說吧。

❏ **Sorry, I have plans.**

不好意思，我有事。

❏ **Sounds good.**

聽起來很好玩欸。

🔍 **關鍵字**

meet up 碰面；會合　　　　**graveyard shift** 大夜班

⚠ **職場成功 Tips**

早班（9 a.m.-5 p.m.）叫 "day shift"，晚班（5 p.m.-12 midnight）叫 "swing shift"。

亨利要開刀，所以接下來兩週會請病假。

🔊 **Track 029**

中式英文　Henry will have an operation, so he'll take a sick leave for the next two weeks.

老外這樣說　**Henry is having an operation, so he'll be out of the office for the next two weeks.**

💡 大師提點

此句要點在於「請病假」的表達方式。"sick leave" 指「病假」，不過在這裡應說成 "he'll be out on sick leave"。（注意，sick leave 前不加冠詞 "a"。）事實上，因開刀 而「短期間內無法上班」更口語的說法是 "he'll be out of the office"。

實境對話

A: **Henry is having an operation, so he'll be out of the office for the next two weeks.**
B: **Oh my gosh. I hope it isn't anything too serious.**

　A：亨利準備要開刀，所以接下來兩週他都不會進辦公室。
　B：我的天哪！希望他的情況不是太嚴重。

老外還會這樣説

❑ Henry is taking a couple weeks off, so we'll all have to pitch in to cover for him.
亨利準備要請幾個星期的假，所以我們要幫忙處理一下他的工作。

❑ Henry is going to take a few personal days. He should be back sometime next week.
接下來幾天亨利會請事假。他在下個星期應該就會回來了。

🔍 **關鍵字**

pitch in 協力；動手做　　　　　　　**take a personal day** 請一天事假

🎧 Track 030

中式英文　Mr. Maguire says strongly that we'll receive 3% extra wages.

老外這樣說　**Mr. Maguire has confirmed that we've all earned a 3% raise.**

Unit
2

 大師提點

中式英文裡的 "Mr. Maguire says strongly …" 聽起來僅有「說」的感覺，並不能用來表示「確認」。若改為 "Mr. Maguire has confirmed …" 便有「已確認（真的會發生）」的意味。另外，「加薪」通常都是以 "pay raise" 或 "salary increase" 來表達，英文並沒有 "receive extra wages" 這種說法。

 實境對話

A: Why are you smiling like that?
B: Mr. Maguire has confirmed that we've all earned a 3% raise.

A：為什麼你笑得那麼開心？
B：麥奎爾先生已經確認我們全都會加薪百分之三。

🔊 **老外還會這樣說**

❏ **Starting next month, you'll be getting a little bump in your paycheck.**
下個月開始你的薪水會往上調一些。

❏ **Congratulations on your promotion. It's well-deserved.**
恭喜升官！那是你應得的。

❏ **Your year-end bonus this year is going to be huge.**
你今年的年終獎金將會非常多。

❏ **Salary adjustments will be made based on your performance review.**
薪資調整將會依照你的績效評核而定。

🔍 **關鍵字**

bump [bʌmp] (n.) 上升；增加　　　**paycheck** [ˋpeˌtʃɛk] (n.) 薪水
year-end bonus 年終獎金　　　**performance review** 績效評核

我問老闆可不可以先預支薪水，但他拒絕了。

🎧 Track 031

中式英文　I asked boss if I can receive my salary beforehand, but he said no.

老外這樣說　**I asked my boss for a salary advance, but he turned me down.**

 大師提點

在英文裡，"salary advance" 就是「預支薪水」的意思，而其中 "advance" 即指「預付款」。至於 "receive salary beforehand" 明顯是中式英文。另外，「回絕／拒絕」使用片語 "turn [someone] down" 來表達會更加道地。

 實境對話

A: You look a little out of it. What's going on?
B: I asked my boss for a salary advance, but he turned me down.

　A：你看起來有點不太對勁。怎麼了？
　B：我向我老闆要求預支薪水，但是被他拒絕了。

📢 **老外還會這樣說**

❏ I asked for a raise, but it's not going to happen.
我要求加薪，但看來是不可能發生了。

❏ I was hoping to be promoted to marketing manager, but they went with someone else.
我希望能被升為行銷經理，但是上面決定的人選不是我。

❏ I just got a terrible performance evaluation.
我的績效被評得非常差。

❏ I just got demoted to a regular sales position.
我剛被降職到一般的業務職位。

🔍 **關鍵字**

out of it 不對勁
turn down 拒絕
performance evaluation 績效評核

salary advance 預支薪資
promote [prə`mot] (v.) 升遷
demote [dɪ`mot] (v.) 降級

Unit 3

會議討論

Meetings

我們開始開會！

🔊 **Track 032**

中式英文 The meeting begins now.

老外這樣說 **Let's get started.**

💡 大師提點

通常在會議開始前，主席會以一句話簡單提醒大家會議要正式開始了。除非是兩三百人的大型研討會，用字遣詞才會比較正式。否則的話，一般在辦公室內的小型會議，就以 "Let's get started."、"Let's begin." 或 "Let's get down to business." 等帶過。

實境對話

A: I think everyone's here.
B: Well, we've got a lot to cover today so let's get started.

A：我想大家都到齊了。
B：嗯，我們今天有很多要討論的事項，所以現在就開始吧。

老外還會這樣說

❏ **I'm going to just go ahead and start.**
我就直接開始了。

❏ **Thank you all for coming.**
謝謝大家前來參與會議。

❏ **We'll start as soon as the projector is ready.**
投影機一準備好，我們就開始。

❏ **We're just waiting for Ms. Tsai to arrive.**
我們在等蔡小姐來。

 關鍵字

cover [ˋkʌvɚ] (v.) 包括；論及
get started 開始；啟動
projector [prəˋdʒɛktɚ] (n.) 投影機

盧法斯先生今天休假，那由誰主持會議呢？

中式英文 Mr. Rufus is not working today. Who will host the meeting?

老外這樣說 **Mr. Rufus is off today. So who will take the chair?**

💡 大師提點

此句為真實例子。筆者在外商公司工作時美國同事問及 "Who will take the chair?" 時，另一台灣同事疑惑：他為什麼要問「誰要搬椅子？」——事實上在此處 "chair" 是「主席席位」的意思，故整句是問「由誰當主席／由誰主持會議？」。類似這種無法從字面上判斷涵義的會議相關詞彙還有 "hold the floor"，意指「擁有發言權」。

實境對話

A: Mr. Rufus is off today. So who will take the chair?
B: I'll do it if no one else wants to.

A：盧法斯先生今天休假，那由誰來主持會議呢？
B：如果沒有其他人想主持的話，就我來吧。

老外還會這樣說

❏ **Whose turn is it to chair the meeting?**
這次輪到誰當會議主席？

❏ **Sharon, could you run the meeting today?**
雪倫，妳可以主持今天的會議嗎？

❏ **Jeff is still in Tokyo, so I'll lead the meeting today.**
傑夫還在東京，所以今天由我來主持會議。

❏ **Ms. Tuban is still out, so why don't we just go around the table?**
圖本小姐還沒回來，所以我們要不要先輪流講一下意見？

🔍 關鍵字

off [ɔf] (*adj.*) 休假的；不上班的
take the chair 主持會議
turn [tɜn] (*n.*) 輪流（機會）
lead [lid] (*v.*) 領導；領先；帶領

Unit
3

本會議將在三點前結束。

🎵 Track 034

中式英文　This meeting will finish before 3:00.

老外這樣說　**The meeting is scheduled to finish by 3:00.**

⚡ 大師提點

一提到「結束」，許多人都會想到直接用 "finish" 一字。這麼說雖然沒錯，但「會議」的召開原本就「安排」好了「預定時程」，何時開始、何時結束通常早已明訂，故使用 "be scheduled to finish ..." 來表達會更貼近原意。

實境對話

A: The meeting is scheduled to finish by 3:00.

B: Well, that would be a first.

A：本會議預計在三點前結束。

B：嗯，那可真是頭一遭了。（言下之意：之前開會從來沒準時結束過。）

老外還會這樣說

❏ **We have to finish before 3:00.**

我們必須在三點前結束。

❏ **Let's keep this meeting under an hour, OK?**

我們將此會議控制在一小時內開完，可以嗎？

❏ **I have another meeting at 3:00, so we'll have to finish before then.**

我三點還有別的會要開，所以我們必須在那之前結束。

❏ **We're not going to leave today until we've reached an agreement.**

除非大家能達成共識，否則今天我們都走不了。

🔍 關鍵字

schedule [ˋskɛdʒʊl] (v.) 預定；安排

reach [ritʃ] (v.) 抵達；達到；與某人取得聯繫

agreement [əˋgrimənt] (n.) 同意；協議

reach an agreement 達成協議

我們接著討論上市策略。

Track 035

中式英文 We're going to discuss the launch strategy.

老外這樣說 **Let's move on to the launch strategy.**

 大師提點

當討論議題有好幾個時，要接續下一個主題，主席應發出 "signal"「訊號」來告知大家現在要討論什麼？此時若使用句型 "Let's move on to + [主題]." 或 "Let's go ahead and talk about + [主題]." 就很明確了。

Unit
3

 實境對話

A: The packaging samples won't be ready until next week.

B: OK, let's move on to the launch strategy.

　　A：包裝樣品要到下週才會準備好。

　　B：好的，那我們先接著討論上市策略。

老外還會這樣說

❏ **Let's move on to the next item.**
　我們接著討論下個議題。

❏ **We're a little behind schedule, so let's move on.**
　我們的進度有點落後，我們加快速度吧。

❏ **I want to talk about the launch strategy now.**
　我想現在來談談產品上市策略。

❏ **Are we ready to discuss the launch strategy now?**
　大家準備好要討論產品上市策略了嗎？

關鍵字

packaging [ˋpækɪdʒɪŋ] (*n.*) 包裝
sample [ˋsæmpl] (*n.*) 樣本；樣品
move on 繼續前進
launch [lɔntʃ] (*n.*) 上市
behind schedule 比預定時間晚

Track 036

中式英文 Miley, what's your idea of this?

老外這樣說 **Do you have any reaction to that, Miley?**

 大師提點

既然是開會，就是希望大家集思廣益，而不是聽一人唱獨角戲。因此，在會議上常會聽到主席詢問與會人士：" John, how do you see this?" 或 "What do you think about that, Judy?" 之類的問題。

 實境對話

A: If we spend our entire budget on online advertising, we won't reach older customers.

B: Do you have any reaction to that, Miley?

A：如果我們將所有的預算都投入網路廣告，那我們就無法接觸到年長的客戶了。

B：麥莉，關於這點妳的看法如何？

老外還會這樣說

❏ **What do you think about that, Miley?**

麥莉，關於這點妳覺得怎麼樣？

❏ **Do you have anything to add to that, Miley?**

麥莉，妳有什麼要補充的嗎？

❏ **Do you want to comment on that, Miley?**

麥莉，妳想對此事發表意見嗎？（我想瞭解妳對此事的看法。）

關鍵字

entire [ɪn`taɪr] (adj.) 所有的；全部的

advertising [`ædvə͵taɪzɪŋ] (n.) 廣告

reaction [rɪ`ækʃən] (n.) 反應

comment [`kɑmɛnt] (v.) 評論

不好意思，我可以插個話嗎？

 Track 037

中式英文　Sorry, can I cut into your talk?

老外這樣說　**Excuse me, may I come in here?**

 大師提點

這句亦是筆者在外商工作期間遇到的真實情況。美國同事想插話便說："May I come in here?" 時，台灣同事便小聲地問我：「他不是已經在會議室了，為何還要說可不可以進來？」──其實這句話意指「可以打個岔嗎？」，是相當普遍、且美國人一聽就明瞭的用法。

 實境對話

A: **If sales continue to decline at this rate, then …**
B: **Excuse me, may I come in here?**

　　A：如果業績照這速度持續下滑，那……
　　B：不好意思，我可以插個話嗎？

📢 **老外還會這樣說**

❏ **Sorry, could I just say something about that?**
對不起，針對此事我可以發表一些意見嗎？

❏ **Excuse me, could I interrupt here just for a second?**
不好意思，我可以打岔一下嗎？

🔍 **關鍵字**

sales [selz] (*n.*) 業績；銷售額
continue [kən`tɪnjʊ] 繼續；持續
rate [ret] (*n.*) 比率；速度；費用
interrupt [͵ɪntə`rʌpt] (*v.*) 中斷；打擾

⚠ **職場成功 Tips**

雖然相較之下老外頗能接受不同意見，但是要打斷他人談話仍須節制，打岔頻率太高的話會令人反感。

Unit
3

Track 038

中式英文 Pardon? Can you repeat it again? I couldn't understand what you're talking about.

老外這樣說 **I'm sorry. Could you please say that again? I didn't quite catch your point.**

大師提點

與老外工作如果有不瞭解的地方，千萬不要不懂裝懂，若因此而讓公事出差錯，老闆可就會說 "Why didn't you just ask?"。另外，台灣同學都習慣將 "repeat" 和 "again" 一起使用，但事實上 "repeat" 一字已有重複的意思，所以不用再接 "again" 囉。

實境對話

A: We need proactive team players to synergize actionable strategies to monetize our deliverables.

B: I'm sorry. Could you please say that again? I didn't quite catch your point.

A：我們需要更積極主動的團隊成員來整合可行的策略，好讓我們的商品能夠賺錢。
B：抱歉。可以麻煩你再講一次嗎？我不太瞭解你的意思。

老外還會這樣說

❏ **I'm sorry. Could you repeat that?**
很抱歉，你可以再講一遍嗎？

❏ **I'm sorry. I didn't hear what you said.**
不好意思，我沒聽清楚你剛說的。

關鍵字

proactive [pro`æktɪv] (adj.) 主動的

actionable [`ækʃənəbḷ] (adj.) 可行的

monetize [`mʌnə͵taɪz] (v.) 使商品等轉化為錢

deliverables [dɪ`lɪvərəbḷz] (n.) 可交貨商品

⚠ 職場成功 Tips

在商場上，事事講求效率，要表達什麼就直接精簡地說明。若試圖要賣弄文采而盡用些艱澀的單字，外籍老闆聽了可能會叫你 "Speak English!"（講白話文！）

我們很快地問一遍看大家是否都同意。

🎵 Track 039

中式英文 Let's have a quick check to see if everybody all wants to do it.

老外這樣說 **Let's go around the table quickly to make sure we all agree.**

 大師提點

開會到一個階段主席要確認大家的意見時，"go around the table" 是相當道地的說法，此即「詢問一輪在會議桌上每一個人的意見」之意。

Unit
3

🧑 **實境對話**

A: It seems that most people think we should relocate the Beijing office.

B: Yes, but let's go around the table quickly to make sure we all agree.

A：看起來大部分同仁都認為我們應該遷移北京辦公室。

B：是的，不過我們還是很快地問一遍看是否大家都同意了。

 老外還會這樣說

❏ **Does anyone have a different opinion?**
有人有不同看法嗎？

❏ **Let's see a quick show of hands. Who agrees with the proposal?**
我們很快地舉手表決一下吧。誰同意此提議案？

❏ **Are we ready to make a decision? Let's go ahead and take a vote.**
我們可以做決定了嗎？我們就直接投票吧。

❏ **Unless there are any objections, let's move ahead with the proposal.**
如果沒有任何異議，我們就照提議案來進行。

🔍 **關鍵字**

show of hands 舉手表決
proposal [prə`pozl] (n.) 提議（案）
objection [əb`dʒɛkʃən] (n.) 反對；異議；妨礙

Track 040

中式英文 | You should receive the meeting records before this Friday.

老外這樣說 | **You should have a copy of the meeting minutes by this Friday.**

大師提點

此例句的重點在於「會議紀錄」這個詞彙。常聽台灣同事說 "meeting records" 或 "meeting notes" 等，但正確的美語用法是 "meeting minutes"，記得 "minute" 要加上 "s"。另外，搭配動詞為 "take"，而 "take the minutes" 就是「做會議紀錄」。

 實境對話

A: Sorry I'm late. What did I miss?
B: You should have a copy of the meeting minutes by this Friday.

A：對不起，我遲到了。我錯過了什麼嗎？
B：你會在本週五前收到會議紀錄。

老外還會這樣說

❏ **I don't think we have to review the minutes from last time.**
我不認為我們需要討論上次的會議紀錄。

❏ **Sam, could you take the minutes today?**
山姆，你可以做今天的會議紀錄嗎？

關鍵字

minutes [`mɪnɪts] (n.) [複數形] 會議紀錄
take the minutes 做會議紀錄

⚠ 職場成功 Tips

會議紀錄內容除了時間、地點、與會者、討論主題等事項外，最重要的是還要包括後續行動 (action items)、負責人 (person in charge) 和完成期限 (deadline) 等，如此開會也才算有達到效果。

中式英文　Let's jump over this problem first.
老外這樣說　**Let's skip this question for now.**

⚡ 大師提點

通常提到「跳過」，大家就立即會想到 "jump" 這個字，但是在此開會情境下所提及的「跳過」某問題，包含「略過」之意，故使用 "skip" 一字較為貼切。

Unit 3

 實境對話

A: Are we going to renew the lease at our Westside location?
B: Let's skip this question for now.

　A：我們要續租在西城的辦公室嗎？
　B：這個問題我們現在先跳過（不討論）。

 老外還會這樣說

❏ **Let's discuss that another time.**
　我們之後再找時間討論這個問題。

❏ **Let's come back to that later.**
　我們等會兒再回頭討論這個問題。

❏ **Let's save that for another time.**
　此議題我們留待以後再討論。

❏ **We don't have time to talk about that now.**
　我們現在沒時間討論此事。

🔍 關鍵字

renew [rɪ`nju] (v.) 繼續；續約
lease [lis] (n.) 租賃
location [lo`keʃən] (n.) 位置；所在地
skip [skɪp] (v.) 跳過；省略
save [sev] (v.) 保留；拯救；儲存；節省

中式英文　I stand by your side.

老外這樣說　**I'll back you up.**

💡 大師提點

此句為相當經典的誤用。中式英文例句裡的 "by your side" 其實是指「陪伴在你身邊」，和「支持／同意」的意思不同，因此並不適合使用於此處。不過，簡單地說："I support you." 也能正確傳達支持之意。

實境對話

A: I'm going to propose going with another distributor.
B: Yeah, I'll back you up.

　　A：我建議我們找另一家經銷商。
　　B：對呀，我支持你。

老外還會這樣說

❑ **I'm with you on that.**
這件事我站你這邊。

❑ **We're in total agreement.**
我們的意見完全一致。

🔍 關鍵字

propose [prə`poz] (v.) 提議；建議
distributor [dɪ`strɪbjətə] (n.) 經銷商
back up 支持

⚠ 職場成功 Tips

若要提出相反意見，美國人通常會先緩和地以 "I see what you mean, but ..." 或 "I can partly agree to that, but ..." 做開場白，然後再接著說出自己的看法。

你們提出的問題，我們一個個處理。

🔊 Track 043

中式英文　We'll deal one-by-one with the questions you offered.

老外這樣說　**Let's deal with the issues you raised one-by-one.**

💡 大師提點

開會中大家急於表達各自的看法而七嘴八舌時，擔任主席者就可以說出這句來請大家按順序討論。其中 "deal with" 是大家熟悉的片語，意指「處理／應付」。此外，"one-by-one" 就是「一個一個地」的意思。

Unit
3

實境對話

A: Basically, the whole project is a mess.

B: Hold on. Let's deal with the issues you raised one-by-one.

　A：基本上，整個專案都亂成一團。

　B：等等（請稍安勿躁）。各位所提出的問題，我們一個個來處理。

老外還會這樣說

❏ **Let's take those one-by-one.**
這些事我們一件一件來處理。

❏ **Let's take a minute to go over your concerns.**
我們花點時間來討論一下你們的疑慮。

❏ **I understand you're frustrated, but let's try to resolve this.**
我瞭解你們很受挫，但是讓我們試著解決這個問題吧。

❏ **I really appreciate your feedback. Let's work this out.**
謝謝你提供寶貴的意見。我們想辦法克服困難吧。

🔍 關鍵字

project [prə`dʒɛkt] (n.) 企劃；專案
hold on 稍等；不掛電話
go over 查看；檢查
frustrated [`frʌstretɪd] (adj.) 受挫的
feedback [`fid,bæk] (n.) 回饋；反應

mess [mɛs] (n.) 混亂；凌亂
issue [`ɪʃju] (n.) 問題；議題
concern [kən`sɜn] (n.) 掛念；關心之事
resolve [rɪ`zɑlv] (v.) 解決
work it out 解決問題；克服困難；加油

🎧 **Track 044**

中式英文　The time is not enough, so can you shorten your talk?

老外這樣說　**We're short of time, so could you be as brief as possible?**

⚡ 大師提點

此句的重點 "short of" 意指「缺乏 / 不足」，因此 "short of time" 即為「時間不足」。而「時間不夠」也可用 "run out of time" 這個片語來表達。另外，請人簡短發言最直接的好用詞是 "be brief"，因為 "brief" 有 "using few words" 的涵義。

實境對話

A: We're short of time, so could you be as brief as possible?
B: Sure, this won't take long.

　A：我們的時間不多了，可以請你長話短說嗎？
　B：好的，我不會講太久。

📢 老外還會這樣説

❑ **We don't have a lot of time, so could you keep it short please?**
　我們並沒有太多時間，可以麻煩你簡單扼要地表達嗎？

❑ **Time is short, so could you just get right to the point?**
　時間不多，請你直接講重點好嗎？

❑ **We don't have a lot of time, so just start with your main point.**
　我們沒有太多時間，所以請直接切入重點。

❑ **I think we're all aware of the problem. What do you suggest we do about it?**
　我想大家都知道問題點了，那你有什麼好的建議？

🔍 關鍵字

short of 短少；不足
brief [brif] (adj.) 簡短的；簡潔的
aware [əˋwɛr] (adj.) 知道的；察覺的

run out of 用盡；耗盡
get right to the point 直接切入重點
be aware of 意識到

下週我們可針對此提議做正式表決。

Track 045

中式英文 Next week we can make an official vote for this proposal.

老外這樣說 **Let's plan to have a formal vote on this proposal next week.**

大師提點

此句的重點在於「正式表決」的說法，也就是 "a formal vote on [something]"。雖然 "official" 這個字在中文裡也可翻譯為「正式的」，但是就語感而言較偏向「官方的 / 法定上的」，故不適宜用在此處。

Unit
3

 實境對話

A: Well, I'd like to thank Cathy for her proposal. It's given us all a lot to think about.

B: Right. Let's plan to have a formal vote on her proposal next week.

　A：嗯，我要感謝凱西的提案。她的提案的確給我們很多啟發。

　B：是的。我們可以在下週針對她的提案做正式表決。

 老外還會這樣說

❏ **Should we just go ahead and vote on it now?**
　我們要不要現在就直接表決？

❏ **Let's think about it and take a vote on it next week.**
　我們都先考慮一下，下週再做表決。

❏ **Do we have a consensus about the best way to proceed?**
　我們對該用什麼方式來進行有共識了嗎？

❏ **Who thinks we should go ahead with the proposal?**
　有誰認為我們應該就依照此提議案進行？

🔍 關鍵字

have/take a vote 投票（表決）
consensus [kən`sɛnsəs] (n.) 共識
proceed [prə`sid] (v.) 繼續進行；開始

我們每兩週開一次會以檢討進度吧。

中式英文 │ Let's have a meeting once in two weeks to check how it's going.

老外這樣說 │ **Let's have a meeting every two weeks to check on progress.**

💡 大師提點

「每兩週一次」不可說成 "once in two weeks"，正確應為 "once every two weeks"，而本句中的「每兩週開一次會」則應說成 "have a meeting every two weeks"。另外，「檢討進度」以 "check on progress" 來表達較為貼近老外的說法。

實境對話

A: We can't afford to have the same kind of delays as we had last time.

B: Right. Let's have a meeting every two weeks to check on progress.

　　A：我們無法承擔像上次那樣的延遲損失。

　　B：沒錯。我們每兩週開一次會以檢討進度吧。

📢 老外還會這樣說

❏ **Let's have a twenty-minute progress meeting every day at 5:30.**
我們每天下午五點半花二十分鐘開個進度討論會吧。

❏ **Let's meet Friday mornings at 9:30 to update everyone on our progress.**
我們週五早上九點半開個會，讓每個人報告一下進度。

❏ **When you say biweekly, do you mean twice a week or once every two weeks?**
當你提到「雙週」，你的意思是一週兩次還是兩週一次？

❏ **To be honest, I think we'd get more done if we had fewer meetings.**
老實說，我認為如果減少開會次數，我們將能夠辦更多事。

🔍 關鍵字

afford [əˋford] (v.) 有足夠的……去做
biweekly [baɪˋwiklɪ] (adj.) 每兩週的；每週兩次的

check on progress 檢討進度
get something done 完成某事

Unit 4

簡報演説

Presentations

我的簡報分四個議題來討論。

中式英文 I'll talk about four topics individually in my presentation.

老外這樣說 **I've divided my presentation into four main sections.**

💡 大師提點

「將簡報分為……部分」可使用 "divide + into" 一詞來傳達「劃分」的感覺。而中式英文當中的 "talk about ... topics" 則僅是一般的描述，相對而言不夠貼切。

實境對話

A: What are you going to talk about today?
B: Well, I've divided my presentation into four main sections.

A：你今天準備談論什麼？
B：嗯，我的簡報分為四個主要部分。

老外還會這樣說

❏ **First, I'll give an overview of the market.**
首先，我會先跟大家報告市場概況。

❏ **Next, I'll talk about the challenges we face.**
接著，我會談一下我們所面臨的挑戰。

❏ **After that, I'll discuss some potential partners.**
之後，我會討論到一些潛在的合作夥伴。

❏ **Finally, I'll make some recommendations.**
最後，我會提供幾點建議事項。

🔍 關鍵字

divide [də`vaɪd] (v.) 劃分
overview [`ovɚ,vju] (n.) 概觀
challenge [`tʃælɪndʒ] (n.) 挑戰
potential [pə`tɛnʃəl] (adj.) 潛在的
recommendation [,rɛkəmɛn`deʃən] (n.) 推薦；建議

🎧 **Track 048**

中式英文　I prepared some copies for you, now please pass them down.

老外這樣說　**I've prepared a handout, which I'll pass around now.**

💡 **大師提點**

「講義、資料」的英文即為 "handout"。將講義「傳／發」下去，則以 "pass around" 來表達。而 "pass down" 其實是「傳承／傳給下一代」的意思！

 實境對話

A: Did you break down revenue by sales region?
B: Yes. I've prepared a handout, which I'll pass around now.

　　A：你有將獲利數字依照業務地區分別表示出來嗎？
　　B：有。我準備了講義，現在發下去給大家。

📢 **老外還會這樣說**

❑ **I have a handout that addresses that. I'll pass it around now.**
　我的講義裡有提到那個部分。我現在將講義發下去。

❑ **Let me pass around a handout that I prepared.**
　我現在把我準備的講義傳下去。

❑ **Please take a look at the handout that I passed around earlier.**
　請看一下我稍早所傳下去的講義。

❑ **On page 2 of the handout I passed around, you'll see a chart with that information.**
　在我所發的講義第二頁，各位可以看到相關資訊的圖表。

🔍 **關鍵字**

break down 將……分類；分解
revenue [ˈrɛvəˌnju] (n.) 收入；利益
region [ˈridʒən] (n.) 區域；地帶
handout [ˈhændaʊt] (n.) 講義；傳單
pass around 傳／發下去
address [əˈdrɛs] (v.) 針對……而說（或寫）；向……發表

若有任何疑問，歡迎隨時提出。

🎵 **Track 049**

中式英文　If there are any questions, please ask me anytime.

老外這樣說　**If you have any questions, please feel free to interrupt.**

💡 大師提點

在老外的口語表達當中，以 "feel free to ask" 或 "feel free to interrupt" 等來邀請提問是很常見的說法，讀者不妨直接記下整個片語，相當實用。

實境對話

A: **How long is your presentation?**

B: **About thirty minutes. If you have any questions, please feel free to interrupt.**

　　A：你的簡報有多長？

　　B：大約三十分鐘。如果你有任何問題，歡迎隨時提出。

📢 老外還會這樣說

❏ **I'd be happy to take questions at any time during my talk.**
在我做簡報時，隨時歡迎提問。

❏ **There will be time for questions at the end.**
在簡報結束後會保留時間給各位問問題。

❏ **I'd like to make this more of a conversation than a presentation, so please jump right in.**
我比較想以討論的方式而不是簡報的方式來進行，所以歡迎隨時提出意見。

❏ **If you have any questions, please don't hesitate to ask.**
如果各位有任何疑問，歡迎提出，別客氣。

🔍 關鍵字

feel free to 隨意；無須拘束
jump in 插話

這張圖表大家看得懂嗎？

🎵 **Track 050**

中式英文 ︱ Does this chart understood by everyone?
老外這樣說 ︱ **Is this chart clear for everyone?**

 大師提點

"Does … understood …?" 為錯誤的被動式組合，正確的用法應該是 "Is … understood …?"。此句說成 "Is this chart clear for everyone?" 最自然。

實境對話

> **A: Is this chart clear for everyone?**
> **B: Not really. What does the red line indicate?**
> A：這張圖表大家看得懂嗎？
> B：不太懂。那條紅線代表什麼？

 老外還會這樣説

❑ **Let me know if you can't see the graph clearly.**
如果有人看不清楚這張圖表，請讓我知道。

❑ **If you can't see the diagram clearly, I'll go ahead and explain it.**
若你們不瞭解此圖表的意義，我會跟大家解釋一下。

❑ **It might be hard to see on this slide, but sales increased slightly in May.**
從這張投影片可能有點難看出來，不過業績在五月份有些許增加。

❑ **The text may be a little too small for everyone to see, so I'll read it quickly.**
字體可能有點小會讓大家看不清楚，所以我很快地唸一次。

🔍 **關鍵字**

chart [tʃɑrt] (n.) 圖表
graph [græf] (n.) 圖解；圖表
slightly [`slaɪtlɪ] (adv.) 稍微地

indicate [`ɪndəˌket] (v.) 表明；指出
diagram [`daɪəˌgræm] (n.) 曲線圖；圖表
text [tɛkst] (n.) 文字；本文

69

這張投影片顯示了過去三年的業績變化。

Track 051

中式英文 This PowerPoint shows the changes of the sales in the past three years.

老外這樣說 **This slide shows the fluctuation of sales over the past three years.**

 大師提點

在商務英語當中，業績的「波動、變化」是以 "fluctuation" 來傳達，而不會直接使用 "change"「改變」這個字。另外，"PowerPoint" 或 "PPT" 是一個電腦程式，不能用來指「投影片」；「投影片」正確的說法是 "slide"。

 實境對話

A: This slide shows the fluctuation of sales over the past three years.
B: Does it include the last two months?
　A：這張投影片顯示了過去三年的業績變化。
　B：包含前兩個月的嗎？

老外還會這樣說

❏ You can see from this slide how much our sales have fluctuated over the past two years.
各位可以從這張投影片看出，過去兩年我們業績變化的幅度。

❏ As you can see here, sales fluctuated wildly over the past three years.
如同各位所見，過去三年業績波動得非常大。

❏ What this slide emphasizes is how inconsistent our sales have been over the past three years.
這張投影片要突顯的是，我們的業績在過去三年相當地不穩定。

🔍 **關鍵字**

fluctuation [ˌflʌktʃʊˋeʃən] (n.) 振盪；波動　　**inconsistent** [ˌɪnkənˋsɪstənt] (adj.) 不一致的

從這些數字各位可看出，市場呈現大幅度的成長。

🎧 Track 052

中式英文 From these numbers, you can find out that the market is rising a lot.

老外這樣說 **As you can see from these figures, the size of the market has increased sharply.**

大師提點

關於市場趨勢變化，像上列中式英文裡的說法 "the market is rising ..." 就是相當經典的因直譯所造成的謬誤。因為，「市場」本身並不會「上揚」；是「市場的大小」會「增加／變大」或「縮減／變小」，因此 "the size of the market has increased ..." 才符合所要表達的意義。

實境對話

A: **How do you explain the sudden jump in revenue?**
B: **As you can see from these figures, the size of the market has increased sharply.**

A：業績突然大幅躍升，你如何解釋？
B：從這些數字各位可以看出，市場規模急劇地成長。

老外還會這樣說

❏ **This graph shows that the size of the market increased sharply.**
此圖表顯示，市場規模成長了不少。

❏ **A look at this chart should help explain the numbers.**
檢視此圖表有助於解釋這些數字的意義。

❏ **The numbers seem to indicate that the market as a whole is growing quickly.**
這些數字似乎顯示出整體市場狀況迅速地在成長當中。

🔍 關鍵字

figure [ˈfɪgjə] (n.) 數字
sharply [ˈʃɑrplɪ] (adv.) 突然地；猛烈地
as a whole 整體看來

這帶出了下一個我想討論的重點。

🎵 Track 053

中式英文 It brings the next point that I'm going to discuss.

老外這樣說 **That brings us to the next point I'd like to make.**

💡 大師提點

> 提到「討論」，許多台灣的英語學習者第一時間會想到 "discuss" 這個字，但是「建立論點 / 提出論點」可以片語 "make a point" 來表達，相對而言感覺更具專業性。

實境對話

A: How much is all this going to cost?
B: Well, that brings us to the next point I'd like to make.

A：做這些事要花多少錢？
B：嗯，這就帶出了我下一個要討論的重點。

📢 老外還會這樣說

❑ Let's take a minute now to look at the costs involved.
現在讓我們花點時間來看一下相關的成本。

❑ I haven't mentioned yet how much all this is going to cost.
我還沒提到這將需要多少費用。

❑ I said earlier that I would talk about costs. I'd like to do that now.
我稍早提到我會討論到成本問題。我現在就來談談。

🔍 關鍵字

involve [ɪnˋvɑlv] (v.) 牽連；涉及；包括
mention [ˋmɛnʃən] (v.) 提及

⚠ 職場成功 Tips

職場上大家都很忙，因此發表簡報時，最好將重點迅速地帶出來，若一直沒有講到核心或答非所問，老闆可能會說 "Don't skirt the issue!"（不要規避問題！）

我想行銷策略部分都討論到了。

🎧 **Track 054**

中式英文　I think I've finished discussing all of the marketing strategy part.

老外這樣說　**I think that covers everything I have to say about our marketing strategies.**

大師提點

「討論完了／該講的都講了」用英文該怎麼說？也許大家直覺會想到 "finish discussing"，但是此詞組的意思其實是「完成討論」，跟原義有所偏離。改用 "cover" 這個字就能表達「含括、涵蓋、包含」等意義，是最道地的說法。

實境對話

A: Do you have anything else you'd like to add?

B: No, I think that covers everything I have to say about our marketing strategies.

A：你還有什麼要補充的嗎？

B：沒有，我想行銷策略的部分我都討論到了。

老外還會這樣說

❏ **That's all I wanted to say about our marketing strategies.**
關於我們的行銷策略，以上就是我的看法。

❏ **I think that's everything I have to say about our marketing strategies.**
我想關於我們的行銷策略，我要講的就是這些了。

❏ **If anyone wants to talk more about marketing strategies, maybe we can get together after the meeting.**
如果在座有人想再多討論一下行銷策略，或許我們可以在會後再聊。

❏ **I think we've spent more than enough time on marketing strategies. Let's move on.**
我想我們已經花夠多時間在討論行銷策略上了。我們繼續下一個議題吧。

🔍 關鍵字

add [æd] (v.) 增加；補充說

🔘 **Track 055**

中式英文   Before discussing about the result of customer research, let's take a break for fifteen minutes.

老外這樣說   **Let's take a fifteen-minute break before we discuss the customer survey results.**

 大師提點

此句要點在於「休息 x 分鐘」。其實很簡單，最直接且自然的說法就是 "Let's take a x-minute break."，其中 x 代表休息的時間，例如 a five-minute break，或是 a twenty-minute break 等。另外，一般的市調應以 "survey" 而非 "research" 表示。

 實境對話

A: **Let's take a fifteen-minute break before we discuss the customer survey results.**
B: **Good idea.**

    A：在討論客戶意見調查結果之前，我們先休息十五分鐘。
    B：好主意。

📣 **老外還會這樣說**

❑ **Let's take a break before getting into the customer survey results. Be back in ten minutes.**
在討論客戶意見調查結果之前，我們先休息一下吧。十分鐘後回來。

❑ **Let's take a fifteen-minute break. We'll start with the customer survey results when we come back.**
我們先休息十五分鐘。回來之後再討論客戶意見調查結果。

❑ **Let's quickly discuss the customer survey results and then take a break.**
讓我們很快地討論一下客戶意見調查結果，然後再休息。

🔍 **關鍵字**

take a break 休息   **survey** [ˋsɝve] (n.) 意見調查
result [rɪˋzʌlt] (n.) 結果   **get into** 開始某事

55 我想 表達 現在歡迎大家針對我的簡報提問。

🎵 Track 056

中式英文 Now you're welcome to make a question about my presentation.

老外這樣說 **Now I'd like to invite your questions regarding my presentation.**

 大師提點

如何用自然又精簡的英文邀請提問？ "You're welcome to make a question" 顯然是中式英文，若改成 "I'd like to invite your questions ..."，就顯得專業、親切多了。

Unit 4

 實境對話

A: **Now I'd like to invite your questions regarding my presentation.**
B: **I have a couple questions.**

　A：現在歡迎大家針對我的簡報內容提問。
　B：我想請問幾個問題。

🔊 **老外還會這樣說**

❑ **Does anyone have any questions?**
任何人有疑問嗎？

❑ **I'd be happy to respond to any comments or questions that anyone has.**
在座各位有任何意見或問題的話，我非常樂意回應。

❑ **If anyone has any questions, I'll do my best to answer them.**
如果各位有任何問題，我會盡力解答。

❑ **Would anyone like to comment on what I talked about this afternoon?**
有人想針對我今天下午所講的主題發表意見嗎？

🔍 **關鍵字**

invite [ɪn`vaɪt] (v.) 邀請；徵求
regarding [rɪ`gɑrdɪŋ] (prep.) 關於；就……而論
respond [rɪ`spɑnd] (v.) 回應；做出反應

你可以針對定價再多做點解釋嗎？

🎵 **Track 057**

| 中式英文 | Can you explain more about the price?
| 老外這樣說 | **Could you expand on this issue of pricing?**

💡 大師提點

談到某個主題而還需要更詳細的討論時，則可以此句型 "Could you expand on this issue of ...?" 來詢問。"explain" 一字雖有「說明、解釋」的意思，但若想表達更深入的討論，應使用 "expand"「擴展、展開、詳述」這個字。

 實境對話

A: Any questions?
B: Yes. Could you expand on this issue of pricing?

　　A：有任何疑問嗎？
　　B：有。你可以針對定價再做些解釋嗎？

 老外還會這樣説

❏ **Could you talk a little more about the pricing?**
你可以針對定價再做些說明嗎？

❏ **Could you go into a little more detail about the pricing?**
你可以針對定價再多做些細節說明嗎？

❏ **Could you explain how you arrived at the prices?**
能不能請你解釋一下這個價格是怎麼算出來的？

❏ **Could you elaborate on what you said earlier about the pricing?**
麻煩你詳細說明一下你稍早提到的價格部分。

🔍 關鍵字

pricing [`praɪsɪŋ] (*n.*) 定價
go into 討論
arrive at 達成
elaborate [ɪˋlæbəˌret] (*v.*) 詳盡闡述

如果我的理解沒錯的話，你想知道這個專案的截止期限，對吧？

🎧 Track 058

中式英文　If I'm right, you want to know when the deadline of the project is, don't you?

老外這樣說　**If I understand you correctly, you want to know the deadline of the project, right?**

💡 大師提點

此句的要點是在釐清聽眾所提問的意思。若要確認自己的認知沒有錯，老外通常會說 "If I understand you correctly …" 來詢問，而非 "If I'm right …"。

實境對話

A: When is all this going to be over and done with?

B: If I understand you correctly, you want to know the deadline of the project, right?

A：這件事什麼時候才會搞定？

B：如果我的認知沒錯的話，你是想知道這個專案的截止期限，對吧？

老外還會這樣說

❏ You're asking about the project deadline. Is that right?
你是在問此專案的截止期限。對不對？

❏ Sorry. I'm not exactly sure what you're asking.
對不起，我不是很確定你這問題的意思。

❏ Are you asking about the meeting today or the project deadline?
你是在問關於今天的會議，還是專案截止日期？

🔍 關鍵字

exactly [ɪgˋzæktlɪ] (adv.) 確切地；精確地

這個問題恐怕超出今天簡報的範圍了。

🔘 **Track 059**

中式英文 I'm afraid your question is out of my presentation today.

老外這樣說 **I'm afraid that question goes beyond the subject of today's presentation.**

 大師提點

當有人在簡報中提到與主題無關的事項時，雖然 "be out of ..." 是指「在……範圍之外」沒錯，但是以片語 "go beyond"「超出……的範圍」來回應會更加貼切。

 實境對話

A: **Do you think we should just close the factory and move production overseas?**

B: **I'm afraid that question goes beyond the subject of today's presentation.**

A：你認為我們應該將工廠關了，然後將生產線遷到海外嗎？

B：這個問題恐怕超出今天簡報的範圍了。

📢 **老外還會這樣說**

❏ **That's a difficult question, and one that's too complex for us to discuss here.**
那個問題很難回答，而且也太複雜了，並不適合在這裡討論。

❏ **That's an important question. What do you think?**
那是個很重要的問題。您的看法如何？

❏ **I'm afraid that's a question for another time.**
恐怕那個問題要另找時間討論。

❏ **I wish we had time today to discuss that, but I don't think we do.**
但願今天我們有時間討論到那個問題，但是我想可能沒辦法。

🔍 **關鍵字**

go beyond 超過某事物的範圍
complex [ˋkɑmplɛks] (*adj.*) 複雜的

🎧 **Track 060**

中式英文   I'm happy to discuss it with you by myself after the presentation.

老外這樣說   **I'd be glad to discuss that with you personally after the presentation.**

 大師提點

"by oneself" 是「獨自」的意思，要表示「親自」應使用 "personally" 才對。

實境對話

A: What's your impression of Mr. Tilton? Do you think he'd be easy to get along with?

B: I'd be glad to discuss that with you personally after the presentation.

　A：你對提頓先生的印象如何？你覺得他好相處嗎？

　B：簡報後我很樂意親自與你討論此事。

 老外還會這樣說

❏ **Maybe we could talk about that during the break.**
或許我們可以等休息時間再聊此事。

❏ **Let's talk about that after the meeting, OK?**
我們會後再討論那件事，好嗎？

❏ **If you don't mind, I'll talk with you about that a little later.**
如果你不介意的話，我稍晚再跟你討論那件事。

❏ **Give me a call sometime and I'll tell you the whole story.**
有空打電話給我，我會跟你講整件事的來龍去脈。

🔍 **關鍵字**

get along with 與……和睦相處
impression [ɪmˋprɛʃən] (n.) 印象
personally [ˋpɝsn̩lɪ] (adv.) 親自；當面

Unit
4

如果你需要進一步討論我剛才所講的內容，請寄 email 給我。

🔘 **Track 061**

中式英文 | If you need to discuss further about what I've just said, please email me.

老外這樣說 | **If you want to follow up on anything I talked about, please email me.**

💡 大師提點

在簡報的尾聲，演講者通常會提到後續聯絡或討論的方式。老外同事經常會說 "follow up on [something] I talked about"，其中片語 "follow up" 帶有「後續採取其他行動」之意，其後再接聯絡方式，例如寄送 email、打電話或另約時間登門拜訪等。

 實境對話

A: **What's the best way to get in touch with you?**
B: **If you want to follow up on anything I talked about, please email me.**

　A：怎麼和你聯絡最方便？
　B：如果你需要進一步討論我剛才所講的內容，請寄 email 給我。

 老外還會這樣說

❏ If anyone wants to discuss this further, please give me a call.
　若有人想更進一步討論這件事，請打電話給我。

❏ If anyone would like to work with me on this, just stop by my office anytime.
　若有人想跟我合作此案，歡迎隨時到我辦公室找我。

❏ If you're interested in learning more, give me your card and I'll get in touch with you.
　如果您有興趣瞭解更多，請給我您的名片，我會跟您聯絡。

🔍 關鍵字
stop by 順道拜訪

Unit 5

電話交談

Telephoning

您好，我是李珊妮。我要找丹佐‧史密斯。

中式英文　Hi. I'm Sunny Lee. May I talk to Denzel Smith?

老外這樣說　**Hi. My name is Sunny Lee. I'm calling for Denzel Smith, please.**

 大師提點

在電話的情境中，因為彼此並沒有真正看到對方，故不用有「兩人面對面交談」感覺的 "I'm ...." 或 "May I talk to ...?" 的說法。打電話時，老外習慣上都會說 "This is/ My name is + [自己的姓名]."、"May I speak to + [對方的姓名]?"，或者是 "I'm calling for + [對方的姓名]." 等。

實境對話

A: **Hi. My name is Sunny Lee. I'm calling for Denzel Smith, please.**
B: **One moment, please.**

　A：您好，我叫李珊妮。麻煩請找丹佐‧史密斯。
　B：請稍等一下。

 老外還會這樣說

❏ Hi. This is Sunny Lee. Is Denzel Smith there?
　您好，我是李珊妮。請問丹佐‧史密斯在嗎？

❏ Hello. Could I speak with Denzel Smith, please?
　您好，麻煩找丹佐‧史密斯。

❏ Hi, this is Sunny Lee from HTC. I'm returning a call from Denzel Smith.
　你好，我是 HTC 的李珊妮。我回電給丹佐‧史密斯。

❏ Hello. Could I have extension 1-4-7, please?
　你好。請幫我轉接分機一四七。

🔍 **關鍵字**

return [rɪˋtɜn] (v.) 送回；返回；回答
return a/someone's call 回電
extension [ɪkˋstɛnʃən] (n.) 延展；電話分機

🎵 Track 063

中式英文　Please hold on. I'm connecting you to his/her extension.

老外這樣說　**Just a moment, please. I'm putting you through.**

 大師提點

為別人「轉接電話」，可使用固定的片語 "put [someone] through" 來表達。其實若要使用 "connect" 這個字亦可，但轉接對象前須接介系詞 "with"，例如："I'll connect you with Mr. Smith."（我幫您轉接給史密斯先生。）

🎧 **實境對話**

A: Just a moment, please. I'm putting you through.
B: Thank you.

　　A：請稍候，我為您轉接。
　　B：謝謝。

Unit
5

📣 **老外還會這樣說**

❑ **Please hold while I transfer your call.**
　請稍候，我為您轉接。

❑ **May I ask who's calling?**
　請問您哪位？

 關鍵字

put someone through 為某人轉接電話

⚠️ **職場成功 Tips**

筆者在外商工作期間，經常幫美國老闆接外國打來的電話。記錄 "caller" 的姓名資訊時，若僅寫 "James"，老闆就會直接問 "James who?"。言下之意就是「這麼多人都叫 James，沒記下姓氏的話，哪會知道是哪個 James 呢？」因此，記錄電話留言時，務必將對方的 "first name"（名）和 "last name"（姓）全都記下喔！

請告訴他溫蒂打電話來過。

🎧 **Track 064**

中式英文　Please tell him that Wendy called.

老外這樣說　**Could you please tell him that Wendy called?**

 大師提點

要麻煩接聽電話者留言和轉達，通常都以「禮貌性地要求」的說法來開頭，像是 "Could you please ...?" 或 "Would you mind ...?" 等，而應避免以直述命令的語氣來要求別人。

 實境對話

A: Would you like to leave a message?
B: Yes, could you please tell him that Wendy called.

A：請問您要留言嗎？
B：好，麻煩您跟他說溫蒂打電話來過。

🔊 **老外還會這樣說**

❏ Just let him know that Wendy called. Thanks.
請轉告他溫蒂打電話來過，謝謝。

❏ No, thanks. I'll try back later.
不用了，謝謝。我稍後再打來。

❏ Could you ask him to return my call as soon as possible? It's very important.
可以麻煩你請他儘速回我電話嗎？這件事非常重要。

❏ Please have her call me back this afternoon after 4:30.
麻煩你請她今天下午四點半之後回我電話。

🔍 **關鍵字**

message [ˋmɛsɪdʒ] (n.)（電話）留言
※ **massage** [məˋsɑʒ] (n.) 按摩〔易混淆〕
leave a message 留言
as soon as possible 儘速；及早

您有空的話，請回電給我。

中式英文　If you have free time, please call back to me.

老外這樣說　**Please call me back when you get a chance.**

 大師提點

「回電」的固定說法就是 "call [someone] back"，而非中式英文裡直譯的 "call back to …"。另外，中文裡「有空的話」若以 "if you have free time" 來表達，會有指「休閒時間」的感覺。在道地的英文口語當中，通常是以 "when you get a chance" 來傳達「有空檔時」之意。

 實境對話

A: I'm sorry. I can't talk right now.

B: Oh, OK. Please call me back when you get a chance.

A：對不起，我現在不方便講話。

B：噢，好的。您有空的話，請回個電話給我。

📢 **老外還會這樣說**

❏ **Oh, OK. Just give me a call when you're free.**

噢，好的。您有空時再打電話給我。

❏ **Oh, OK. I'll call you back later.**

噢，好的。我稍後再打給您。

⚠ **職場成功 Tips**

跟老外溝通時，最注重的是明確、直接，避免語意模糊的句子。例如，如果只說 "I'll contact you soon."（我很快會跟你聯絡。），老外心裡會想 "How? And when?"（如何聯絡？很快是多快？）不如將細節直接說出，像是 "I'll call you this afternoon around 3:00."（我今天下午三點左右會打電話給你。），就可以避免誤會了。

您現在方便講話嗎？

Track 066

中式英文 Are you convenient to answer the phone now?

老外這樣說 **Is now a good time to talk?**

大師提點

既然電話都已經接通了，此時再問對方是否可以 "answer the phone" 便顯得不合理。另外，「是否方便」也絕不能以直譯方式 "Are you convenient ..." 來敘述，因為 "convenient" 這個字不能以「人」為對象。

實境對話

A: Hello. This is Max.
B: Hi, Max. It's Catlin. Is now a good time to talk?

A：你好。我是麥克思。

B：嗨，麥克思。我是凱特琳。你現在方便講話嗎？

老外還會這樣說

❏ **Can you talk now?**

你現在可以講電話嗎？

❏ **I hope I haven't caught you at a bad time.**

希望我打這通電話沒打擾到你。

❏ **Sorry to bother you again. Do you have a couple minutes?**

不好意思又要打擾你。你現在有幾分鐘的時間嗎？

🔍 關鍵字

catch someone at a bad time 在某人不方便時與他 / 她談話
bother [`bɑðə] (v.) 打擾；使惱怒；使困擾

⚠ 職場成功 Tips

商務人士都相當忙碌，既然會問接聽者是否有空講話，就該知道時間寶貴，應直接講重點。之前筆者有個同事很喜歡在接通電話之後，先問 "Hey, Lily. Can you talk now? OK, so how was your weekend?"（嗨，莉莉，妳現在方便講話嗎？好，那……妳週末過得如何？）像這樣，不直接講要點的話，會讓人感到莫名其妙。

中式英文 I can't hear you clearly. Could you say it louder?

老外這樣說 **I can hardly hear you. Could you speak up?**

 大師提點

電話聽不清楚時請對方「大聲」一點，不應使用中文直譯的 "say it louder"，而應藉由片語 "speak up" 來傳達。另外，若說 "I can't hear you clearly."，老外也聽得懂，不過改用 "hardly" 一字來代表 "almost not"（幾乎不），則顯得更加道地。

 實境對話

A: I can hardly hear you. Could you speak up?
B: Oh, sure.

　A：您講什麼我聽不清楚。可以說大聲一點嗎？
　B：噢，好的。

📢 **老外還會這樣說**

❏ **Sorry, I didn't get that. It's a little noisy here.**
不好意思，我剛沒聽清楚。這裡有點吵雜。

❏ **Could you speak a little more slowly, please?**
可以請您再講慢一點嗎？

🔍 **關鍵字**

hardly [ˋhɑrdlɪ] (adv.) 幾乎不；簡直不
speak up 大聲說

⚠️ **職場成功 Tips**

筆者之前有個加拿大籍的老闆，每次打電話到我的手機時，接通後的第一句話總是 "Wendy, can you hear me clearly?"，確認手機通訊正常後才開始說明來電用意。如果聽不太清楚，他就會說："Let me call you right back."（我現在馬上重撥一次。）

67 我想表達　太扯了！我已經在電話上等了快五分鐘了。

🎵 **Track 068**

中式英文　It's ridiculous. I've been waiting on the line for almost five minutes.

老外這樣說　**This is outrageous. I've been on hold for nearly five minutes.**

💡 **大師提點**

這句的重點在於我們中文裡常說的「很扯 / 太誇張」該如何表達。"ridiculous" 的意思是「荒唐的 / 可笑的」。但此處的情境是「因在線上等太久而有點惱怒」，故應使用 "outrageous" 才比較能夠傳達「太過分、太誇張了吧！」的感覺。另外，"put [someone] on hold" 即指「讓某人在電話線上等候」。

 實境對話

A: **This is outrageous. I've been on hold for nearly five minutes.**
B: **I apologize for the long wait. Calls are taken in the order they are received. How may I help you?**

A：太過份了！我已經在電話上等了快五分鐘了。
B：很抱歉讓您久等了。我們都是依照來電順序接聽的。有什麼我可以為您服務的嗎？

📢 **老外還會這樣説**

❏ **This is the third time I've been put on hold.**
這已經是第三次要我在線上等了。

❏ **Do *not* put me on hold again.**
不要再讓我在線上等了！

🔍 **關鍵字**

outrageous [aʊtˋredʒəs] (*adj.*) 極不合理的　　**on hold** 暫停；暫不處置
apologize [əˋpɑləˌdʒaɪz] (*v.*) 道歉　　**receive** [rɪˋsiv] (*v.*) 收到；接到

88

我現在在電話上。兩分鐘之後再回電給您可以嗎?

中式英文 I'm talking to someone else on the other phone. I'll call you back in two minutes, OK?

老外這樣說 **I'm afraid I'm on the other line. Can I call you back in two minutes?**

💡 大師提點

有時電話進來,我們可能正好在講另一通電話,此時直接說 "I'm on the other line." 就能明確地表示「此刻正在另一條線上」。說明狀況後,再利用 "Can I call you back in [number] minutes?" 這個句型主動告知回電時間則更加周到。

 實境對話

Unit
5

A: Hi, pumpkin! It's mom!
B: I'm afraid I'm on the other line. Can I call you back in two minutes?

　　A:我的小乖乖!我是媽媽啊!
　　B:我現在在電話上。兩分鐘後回電給妳可以嗎?

 老外還會這樣說

❏ **Sorry, I can't talk now. Can I call you back?**
抱歉,我現在不方便講話。可以稍後回電給您嗎?

❏ **Could you hold on a second? I'm on the other line.**
您可以稍等一下嗎?我現在正在另外一通電話上。

❏ **I'm kind of in the middle of something. I'll call you back soon, OK?**
我現在手邊在忙別的事。我很快再回你電話,可以嗎?

❏ **Sorry, this isn't a good time to talk. Could you try back later?**
對不起,我現在不方便講電話。能不能請你等會兒再打?

🔍 關鍵字

pumpkin [`pʌmpkɪn] (*n.*) [口語] 暱稱小孩,「小乖乖 / 小可愛」之意。
kind of 有一點
in the middle of something 正在忙著做某事

不好意思，就先這樣。我要接另一通電話了。

Track 070

中式英文　Sorry, I must hang up on you now. Another phone is ringing.

老外這樣說　**Sorry, I have to go now. Someone is calling on the other line.**

 大師提點

若正在忙又剛好遇到煩人的電話，就說 "I've got to go." 來打發吧。中式英文裡的 "hang up on [someone]" 是指「掛某人電話」，而 "Another phone is ringing." 則完全是「另一支電話在響了」的逐字直譯，事實上老外並不會這樣表達！

 實境對話

A: In addition to health insurance, we also offer life and auto.

B: Sorry, I have to go now. Someone is calling on the other line.

A：除了健康保險之外，我們還提供壽險和車險。

B：不好意思，就先這樣。我現在要接另一通電話。

📢 **老外還會這樣說**

❑ **Sorry, I have another call. Thank you and good-bye.**
不好意思，我還有電話在線上。謝謝，再見。

❑ **Sorry, I've got a call coming in on the other line.**
不好意思，我有另一線電話進來了。

❑ **Thanks, but I'm just not interested.**
謝謝，但是我沒興趣。

❑ **Sorry, I'm in a meeting. Good-bye.**
不好意思，我在開會。再見。

🔍 **關鍵字**

in addition to 除了……還有

insurance [ɪnˋʃʊrəns] (n.) 保險

auto [ˋɔto] (n.) 汽車

我重複一次，以確認我記下的是正確資訊。

中式英文 　Let me repeat it again to make sure that what I'm writing is correct.

老外這樣說 **Let me repeat that to make sure I got it.**

⚡ 大師提點

"What I'm writing ..." 是以直譯方式翻出「我所寫的東西」，但此處並不是在寫什麼文章，僅是記錄一些資訊罷了，故用 "that" 和 "it" 精簡表達即可。

實境對話

A: Ask her to call Mr. Lee at 0930-466-0646 after 4:00 but before 6:00.

B: Let me repeat that to make sure I got it.

A：請她在四點以後六點以前打電話到 0930-466-0646 找李先生。

B：我重複一次，以確認我記下的是正確資訊。

老外還會這樣說

❏ **Could you repeat that number, please?**

可以麻煩您再講一次那個號碼嗎？

❏ **Let me read that back to you. It's 0930-466-0646. Is that right?**

讓我重複一次給你聽。是 0930-466-0646，沒錯吧？

❏ **Sure. Is your name spelled L-E-E or L-I?**

沒問題。您的名字是拼成 L-E-E 還是 L-I 呢？

❏ **Could you spell your name, please?**

可以麻煩您把名字拼出來嗎？

🔍 關鍵字

get it 懂得；瞭解

spell [spεl] (v.) 拼字；拼寫

我打電話來是想約明天的開會時間。

🎵 Track 072

中式英文　I call because I want to make an appointment for the meeting
tomorrow.

老外這樣說　**I'm calling to arrange a meeting for tomorrow.**

 大師提點

說明來電目的可以使用句型 "I'm calling to + V."，或者是 "I'm calling about + N." 來
表達。像中式英文裡的 "I call because I want to ..."，老外根本不會這麼說！另外，
"make an appointment" 是指「約定會面、看診」等之意。

 實境對話

A: May I ask what your call is concerning?
B: I'm calling to arrange a meeting for tomorrow.
　　A：可以請問您打這通電話有什麼事嗎？
　　B：我打電話來是想約明天的開會時間。

🔊 **老外還會這樣說**

❏ **I'm returning Mr. Liu's call.**
我是回電給劉先生。

❏ **I'm calling about Mr. Chang's order.**
我打電話來是要問有關張先生訂單的事。

❏ **I just want to confirm that someone will meet me at the airport when
I arrive.**
我只是想確認一下我抵達機場時會有人在那接我。

❏ **I'm calling because I won't be able to attend the meeting tomorrow.**
我打這通電話是要告知您我明天無法參加會議。

🔍 **關鍵字**

arrange [əˋrendʒ] (v.) 安排
order [ˋɔrdə] (n.) 命令；訂單；順序
confirm [kənˋfɜm] (v.) 確認
attend [əˋtɛnd] (v.) 出席

我想打一通對方付費電話到休士頓。

Track 073

中式英文 I want to make a call to Houston and the answering person will pay for me.

老外這樣說 **I'd like to place a collect call to Houston, please.**

大師提點

很多人都知道「免付費電話」叫 "toll-free number"，但對於 "collect call"「對方付費電話」卻很陌生。這句話其實很簡單，若是用像中式英文裡的句子那般冗長的解釋，老外反而會聽不懂呢！

 實境對話

A: I'd like to place a collect call to Houston, please.
B: Please enter the number you are trying to reach.

A：麻煩你，我想打一通對方付費電話到休士頓。
B：請輸入您想接通的電話號碼。

 老外還會這樣說

❏ **Hello, operator. I'd like make a collect call.**
喂，接線生。我想打一通對方付費電話。

❏ **Please state your name at the tone.**
請在撥號音之後說出您的姓名。

❏ **You have a collect call from "Iris." Will you accept the charges?**
有一位叫「愛瑞思」的人打了一通對方付費電話給您。請問您願意付費接聽嗎？

❏ **I'll accept the charges.**
我願意付費接這通電話。

關鍵字

operator [`ɑpə,retə] (n.) 接線人員
state [stet] (v.) 陳述；說明
tone [ton] (n.)（電話裡表示可撥號的）撥號音 [=dial tone]

🎵 **Track 074**

中式英文 My cell phone is running out of battery.

老外這樣說 **My battery is nearly out.**

⚡ 大師提點

片語 "run out of [something]" 意指「某（貯存）物品耗盡」，而此處「手機電池沒電」，在美國一般都是說 "My battery is nearly out."，或使用 "dead"、"die" 來表示「電力不足」。

實境對話

A: My battery is nearly out.
B: OK, give me a call back when you can.
　A：我手機快沒電了。
　B：好，你方便的時候再回電給我。

老外還會這樣說

❑ **My phone is about to die.**
　我手機快沒電了。

❑ **My battery is about to go dead.**
　我手機電池快沒電了。

❑ **I need to save my battery. I'll call you back when I get to the office.**
　我得省著點用電池的電力。我到辦公室再打電話給你。

🔍 關鍵字

battery [ˋbætərɪ] (n.) 電池
be about to 即將；正要
die [daɪ] (v.) 死；（機械）停轉；（電池）沒電
go dead 電池耗盡電力
get to 抵達；開始

我要進電梯了，收不到訊號。

🎵 **Track 075**

中式英文　I'm entering the elevator, so I won't receive the connection.

老外這樣說　**I'm going into an elevator. I'm going to lose you.**

 大師提點

在英文口語當中，"lose you" 就是「收不到訊號」的意思！非常道地也很傳神，傳達出「我們之間的連結斷線」的感覺。另外，「進電梯」簡單地說 "go into an elevator" 即可，若使用 "enter the elevator" 反而顯得不自然。

實境對話

A: I'm going into an elevator. I'm going to lose you.

B: OK. Talk to you soon.

　A：我要進電梯了，會收不到訊號。

　B：好，等會兒再說。

 老外還會這樣說

❑ **I'll call you back in a few minutes.**
我幾分鐘之後再打電話給你。

❑ **I think we've got a bad connection. Let me call you back, OK?**
我想是收訊不良。我再重打一次給你，好嗎？

❑ **I'm getting terrible reception here. Let me go outside.**
這裡收訊非常差。我去外面接。

❑ **The signal here is terrible. I've only got one bar.**
這裡訊號很弱。我的手機訊號只有一格。

🔍 **關鍵字**

elevator [ˈɛləˌvetə] (n.) 電梯
connection [kəˈnɛkʃən] (n.) 連接；連線
terrible [ˈtɛrəbl] (adj.) 極糟糕的；可怕的
reception [rɪˈsɛpʃən] (n.)（訊號）接收
signal [ˈsɪgnl] (n.) 訊號；信號

Unit
5

Unit 6

★ ★ ★ ★ ★ ★ ★ ★ ★ ★ ★ ★ ★ ★ ★ ★ ★ ★ ★

面試問答

Interviews

這是我的榮幸。我一直期待和您談一談。

中式英文　It's my pleasure. I always want to talk to you.

老外這樣說　**The pleasure's all mine. I'm really looking forward to talking with you.**

 大師提點

"It's my pleasure." 這句話並無錯誤，但是通常使用在回應他人道謝時，意味著「我很樂意提供協助」。而在此面試情境中所要表達的「能有機會跟老闆會面，我倍感榮幸。」，則應使用 "The pleasure's all mine." 才正確。另外，若只是說 "want to" 無法傳遞「期待」的感覺，改用 "look forward to" 的話就貼切許多。

 實境對話

A: Hello, Ms. Wu. I'm Steve McClusky. Nice to meet you.

B: The pleasure's all mine. I'm really looking forward to talking with you.

A：吳小姐，您好。我是史蒂夫‧麥肯克斯基，很高興見到您。

B：這是我的榮幸。我一直期待能跟您談一談。

📢 老外還會這樣說

❏ Thank you very much for meeting with me.
非常感謝您撥冗和我見面。

❏ Hello, Mr. McClusky. It's so nice to finally meet you in person.
麥肯克斯基先生，您好。很開心終於能親自與您見面。

❏ Hello, Mr. Young. How are you doing?
嗨，楊先生。你好嗎？

🔍 關鍵字

pleasure [ˋplɛʒɚ] (n.) 榮幸；愉快的事

in person 親自

我在行銷管理方面有相當多的實戰經驗。

🔊 **Track 077**

中式英文 I have many practical experiences in marketing management.

老外這樣說 **I've got a lot of hands-on experience in marketing management.**

 大師提點

首先，"experience" 一字當「經驗」解釋時是不可數名詞，複數字尾不加 "s"；若指「閱歷、經歷過某事件」才是可數名詞。而在此處為「經驗」之意，故不可數。另外，雖然 "practical" 一字也包括「有用的／實際的」的意思，但是在這裡改用 "hands-on" 這個形容詞則更能強調「實際動手做過」的意涵。

 實境對話

A: What kind of management experience do you have?

B: I've got a lot of hands-on experience in marketing management.

A：您在管理方面有什麼樣的經驗？

B：我在行銷管理方面有很多實戰經驗。

Unit 6

🧑‍🦰 **老外還會這樣說**

❑ **I have a strong background in managing manufacturing operations.**
我在管理生產運作方面有很深厚的經歷。

❑ **I've mostly managed small creative teams.**
我主要是帶領小型的創意團隊。

🔍 **關鍵字**

management [ˋmænɪdʒmənt] (n.) 管理

hands-on experience 實際上手經驗

manufacturing [ˌmænjəˋfæktʃərɪŋ] (adj.) 製造的

experience [ɪkˋspɪrɪəns] (n.) 經驗；閱歷

background [ˋbækˌɡraʊnd] (n.) 背景；經歷

⚠️ **職場成功 Tips**

面試時免不了會討論到自己過去的工作經驗。"I've got a lot of hands-on experience in [something]." 此句型只要加以靈活運用，就能簡潔明瞭地讓雇主瞭解自己的專業領域。

我可能有點完美主義，所以有時候我會過於注重細節。

中式英文 Maybe I'm a little picky, so I care too much about the details sometimes.

老外這樣說 **I tend to be a bit of a perfectionist, so sometimes I pay too much attention to details.**

💡 **大師提點**

面試中通常會討論到求職者的優缺點。談優點當然沒問題，但是談缺點的話，就要技巧性地提一個聽起來並非太嚴重的問題。中式英文裡 "picky" 一字的涵義包括「吹毛求疵／機車／龜毛」等，給人過於負面的感覺，說了反而對自己無益。老外通常會用 "tend to"「傾向」來傳達程度較低的事情，而最重要的是，"perfectionist"「完美主義者」並不是什麼非常糟糕的缺點，再加上運用片語 "pay too much attention to [something]" 來表達「過於注重某事」就是相當自然的說法。

 實境對話

A: **What would you say is your greatest weakness?**
B: **I tend to be a bit of a perfectionist, so sometimes I pay too much attention to details.**
　A：你認為你最大的缺點是什麼？
　B：我可能有點完美主義，所以有時候會太注重細節。

 老外還會這樣説

❏ **I sometimes stretch myself too thin by taking on too many tasks.**
我有時會攬太多事情在身上，而把自己逼得太緊。

❏ **My background is corporate sales rather than consumer sales, but I think that there's quite a bit of overlap.**
我是學企業銷售出身的，而不是消費性產品銷售，不過我認為兩者之間有很多共通點。

🔍 **關鍵字**

stretch someone too thin 把某人逼得太緊　　**corporate** [`kɔrpərɪt] (*adj.*) 公司的
consumer [kən`sjumə] (*n.*) 消費者　　**overlap** [ˌovə`læp] (*n.*) 重疊

我有強烈的意願和動力學習。

中式英文 I have the strong will and energy to learn.

老外這樣說 **I have a strong willingness and drive to learn.**

 大師提點

在中式英文裡，"will" 一字是指「意志／自制力」，比方說："Mary has a weak will."（瑪麗是個意志力薄弱的人。）而 "energy" 的字義較偏向「精力／活力」。比方說："I drink Red Bull to get some quick energy."（我喝提神飲料快速補充體力。）兩者所構成的語意皆與中文要表達的意思有所偏離。此處所提到的學習「意願」和「動力」分別使用 "willingness" 及 "drive" 這兩個字來表示會更符合老外平常的用語。

 實境對話

A: Is there anything else you think I should know about you?
B: I have a strong willingness and drive to learn.

A：你還有什麼其他想補充、可以讓我更瞭解你的嗎？
B：我有強烈的意願和動力學習。

Unit
6

🗣 **老外還會這樣說**

❏ **I'm constantly learning new skills so that I can be more effective in my work.**
我持續不斷地在學習新的技能，好讓自己在工作上表現得更好。

❏ **I pick things up very quickly, so I'm confident I could begin making a contribution right away.**
我學東西很快，所以我有信心可以很快地為公司做出貢獻。

🔍 **關鍵字**

willingness [ˋwɪlɪŋnɪs] (*n.*) 意願　　　　**drive** [draɪv] (*n.*) 動力
effective [ɪˋfɛktɪv] (*adj.*) 有效的；好的　　**pick up something** 學會某事

我希望在可以自我成長，同時也能做出長期貢獻的地方工作。

中式英文　I hope to work in the place that I can grow up and also make long-term contributions.

老外這樣說　**I'm definitely looking for a place where I can grow and make a long-term contribution.**

💡 大師提點

就語感而言，"I hope to ..." 的說法無法強調出自信感，聽起來好像僅是「希望可以」而已。相反地，若是使用 "I'm definitely looking for ..." 聽起來就堅定多了，面試時這樣說較能為自己加分。另外，"grow up" 是指「長大」，例如 "My girls grew up."（我女兒長大了。），若要表達「成長」，使用 "grow" 即可。

實境對話

A: What kind of company do you want to work for?
B: I'm definitely looking for a place where I can grow and make a long-term contribution.

A：你希望在何種類型的公司上班？
B：我當然希望在可以自我成長，同時也能做出長期貢獻的地方工作。

老外還會這樣說

❏ **I think somewhere with a fast-paced work culture would be a good match for me.**
我想具有快步調工作文化的公司比較適合我。

🔍 關鍵字

definitely [ˋdɛfənɪtlɪ] (adv.) 確切地；當然　　**long-term** [ˋlɔŋ͵tɝm] (adj.) 長期的

contribution [͵kɑntrəˋbjuʃən] (n.) 貢獻　　**fast-paced** [ˋfæst͵pest] (adj.) 快節奏的

⚠ 職場成功 Tips

對於工作許多人都希望「錢多、事少、離家近」，但是在面試應答時，必須為老闆和公司的利益著想，強調自己可以為公司做出什麼貢獻，才有機會雀屏中選。

我在週末喜歡看電影、聽音樂，不過我也非常喜歡瑜伽。

🎵 Track 081

中式英文　I like to watch movies, listening to the music on the weekend. However, I do yoga very often.

老外這樣說　**On the weekends, I enjoy movies and music, but I'm also a big fan of yoga.**

  大師提點

老外經常使用 "enjoy" 這個字來表達「欣賞／喜愛／得到樂趣」，比起 "like"「喜歡」更生動。另外，台灣同學很習慣說 "I do [something] very often."，其實換個說法改說 "I'm a big fan of [something]." 將會更道地，不僅能傳達「經常做」的意思，同時也讓聽者知道你樂在其中。

👓 **實境對話**

A: **What do you like to do when you're not working?**
B: **On the weekends, I enjoy movies and music, but I'm also a big fan of yoga.**

　　A：你沒上班時都喜歡做些什麼？
　　B：週末時，我喜歡看電影和聽音樂，不過我也非常喜歡瑜伽。

  老外還會這樣說

❑ I spend as much time as I can outdoors—hiking and mountain biking mostly.
我只要有時間就會做戶外活動，主要是登山和騎越野自行車。

🔍 **關鍵字**

outdoors [ˋautˋdorz] (*adv.*) 在戶外　　　　**hiking** [haɪkɪŋ] (*n.*) 登山健行

⚠ **職場成功 Tips**

老闆想聘請的員工應該是身心都健康的人。因此，面談時若被問及休閒活動，最好能舉出一兩樣運動或正當興趣。千萬不要說「連週末都在加班」這種試圖討好老闆的話，否則可能弄巧成拙。

我自認是有熱情、勤奮的員工，而且我很懂得如何與人相處。

🎧 Track 082

中式英文 | I think I'm a passionate and hard-working worker. In addition, I love to hang out with people.

老外這樣說 | **I consider myself to be a passionate, diligent worker, and I have exceptional interpersonal skills.**

💡 大師提點

雖然 "think" 也是「認為」的意思，但是 "consider" 一字包含「將……視為」的涵義，在像面試這樣較正式的場合中使用會顯得更得宜。另外，片語 "hang out with [someone]" 是指「跟 [某人] 出去玩樂」，和此處所提到的「與人相處」意思不同。

實境對話

A: **Why do you think you're the best candidate for the job?**

B: **I consider myself to be a passionate, diligent worker, and I have exceptional interpersonal skills.**

A：你為什麼認為你是這份工作的最佳人選？

B：我自認是一個有熱情、勤奮的員工，而且我很懂得如何與人相處。

老外還會這樣說

❏ **From everything you've told me, I think my skills and experience are a perfect match for the position.**

從您前面所做的介紹，我認為我的技能和經驗非常適合這個職位。

❏ **I'm a very good salesperson with a proven track record of generating revenue.**

我是一個非常優秀的業務人員，我擁有足以證明能幫公司獲利的業績紀錄。

🔍 關鍵字

candidate [ˋkændədet] (n.) 求職應徵者

diligent [ˋdɪlədʒənt] (adj.) 勤奮的

track record 過去的業績；紀錄

passionate [ˋpæʃənɪt] (adj.) 有熱情的

interpersonal [ˌɪntɚˋpɜsənl] (adj.) 人際的

generate [ˋdʒɛnəˌret] (v.) 產生

🎧 **Track 083**

中式英文　In addition to the knowledge, I learned a lot of practical skills too.

老外這樣說 **Besides the theoretical knowledge, I also learned a lot of practical skills.**

💡 **大師提點**

「除了……之外，還有……」用 "in addition to" 比用 "besides" 來得生硬。另外，中式英文裡僅提到 "knowledge"「知識」還不夠清楚。此處要強調的是「理論知識」，故應以 "theoretical knowledge" 區隔和 "practical skills"「實務技巧」的差異。

 實境對話

A: Do you think your academic training has prepared you for this position?

B: Yes. Besides the theoretical knowledge, I also learned a lot of practical skills.

　A：你認為你在學校所受過的訓練可以讓你勝任這個職務嗎？
　B：是的。除了理論之外，我也學到很多實務技巧。

 老外還會這樣說

❏ I think so. I have strong grounding in theory that I think I can apply to a lot of different situations.

　我認為可以。我有深厚的理論基礎，我認為我能將它應用到各種不同的情況上。

❏ Yes, my program emphasized practice much more than theory.

　是的，我所學的課程都強調實務重於理論。

❏ To be honest, I think my work experience is far more relevant.

　老實說，我認為我的工作經驗更具相關性。

🔍 **關鍵字**

academic [ˌækəˈdɛmɪk] (adj.) 學術性的
practical [ˈpræktɪkl̩] (adj.) 實際的；實務的
apply to 適用於

theoretical [ˌθiəˈrɛtɪkl̩] (adj.) 理論上的
grounding [ˈgraʊndɪŋ] (n.) 基本訓練；底子
relevant [ˈrɛləvənt] (adj.) 切題的；關係重大的

我的強項之一是我適應新環境的能力很好。

🎵 **Track 084**

中式英文 One of my merits is I have the ability to adapt to new environment very well.

老外這樣說 **One of my biggest advantages is my ability to adapt well to new situations.**

💡 大師提點

「強項」到底該怎麼說呢？雖然 "merit" 可指「優點」，但是其語感較偏向 "value" 或 "worth"「價值」。在此情境中用 "advantage" 一字說明自己的「優勢」比較自然。另外，"one of my biggest advantages ..." 聽起來有「很多強項的其中一個」的感覺，在面試時是相當具技巧性的說法。

 實境對話

A: **In what type of setting do you perform the best?**
B: **One of my biggest advantages is my ability to adapt well to new situations.**
　A：你在何種情況下表現最佳？
　B：我的強項之一是我適應新環境的能力很好。

 老外還會這樣說

❏ **I've worked quite effectively in several very different work environments.**
我曾在幾個相當不同的環境下工作，但是表現得都很優異。

❏ **I'm very organized, which allows me to effectively prioritize the tasks I have to accomplish.**
我做事很有條理，這點讓我能夠有效地將必須完成的工作設定優先順序。

🔍 關鍵字

perform [pɚ`fɔrm] (v.) 表演；表現
adapt [ə`dæpt] (v.) 適應
prioritize [praɪ`ɔrə͵taɪz] (v.) 設定優先順序
advantage [əd`væntɪdʒ] (n.) 優勢
organized [`ɔrgən͵aɪzd] (adj.) 有條理的
accomplish [ə`kɑmplɪʃ] (v.) 完成

過去兩年內，我成功地實行了有效的系統並產生出潛在客戶名單。

中式英文　In the past two years, I successfully carried out a valid system and produced a potential customer list.

老外這樣說　**Over the past two years, I successfully implemented a very effective system for generating sales leads.**

大師提點

首先，使用 "Over the past two years, ..." 有「過去兩年來」的意味。另外，"carry out" 雖有「實行」之意，但使用 "implement" 較專業。最後，商業界的「產生潛在客戶」有其固定說法："generate sales leads"，這可說是商務人士的必備術語。

實境對話

A: Tell me about what you consider your most significant accomplishment?

B: Over the past two years, I successfully implemented a very effective system for generating sales leads.

A：說說你認為你最大的成就是什麼？

B：過去兩年內，我成功地實行了一個非常有效的系統並產生出潛在客戶名單。

Unit 6

老外還會這樣説

❏ I'm probably most proud of a system that I created to generate sales leads.

我設計了可產生潛在客戶的系統，我想這應該是最讓我感到自豪的事。

❏ My accomplishments mostly involve reengineering systems to make them simpler and cheaper.

我的成就主要包括改造工程系統，我讓它們變得更簡易而且更省成本。

關鍵字

significant [sɪgˋnɪfəkənt] (adj.) 重大的　　　**sales leads** 潛在客戶；銷售線索

那是個很棒的經驗，因為我克服了種種困難。

🎧 **Track 086**

| 中式英文 | That was a great experience because I overcame variety of difficulties. |

| 老外這樣說 | **It was a wonderful experience because I really thrive on challenges.** |

💡 **大師提點**

要形容「很棒的」用 "wonderful" 比 "great" 來得強烈與興奮。另外，「克服困難」按字面順序翻成 "overcome difficulties" 雖然並沒有什麼錯誤，但是顯得較無變化。如果改說 "thrive on challenges" 還能帶出「克服了挑戰變得更茁壯」的語感。

 實境對話

A: Can you tell me a little bit about your previous position?
B: It was a wonderful experience because I really thrive on challenges.

A：能不能請你稍微談一談你的前一份工作？
B：那是個很棒的經驗，因為我克服了種種挑戰也成長很多。

 老外還會這樣說

❏ **It was an excellent opportunity for me to become an expert in mobile advertising.**
那對我來說是個絕佳的機會，讓我變成了行動廣告的專家。

❏ **It was a great chance for me to implement a lot of new user-interface ideas that I'd been working on.**
那是個很棒的機會，讓我一直在策劃的一些使用者介面的點子能夠付諸實行。

🔍 **關鍵字**

thrive [θraɪv] (*v.*) 茁壯；成長　　　　　**mobile** [ˋmobɪl] (*adj.*) 行動的

⚠ **職場成功 Tips**

工作上一定會遇到困難，重要的是處理困難的態度。被問到過去的工作經驗，絕對不要說前公司或老闆的壞話，而應該將過去所遇到的困難都當成是讓自己進步的寶貴經驗。

這問題很有趣。給我點時間想想怎麼回答。

Track 087

中式英文　That's an interesting question. Give me some time and think about the answer.

老外這樣說　**That's an interesting question. Give me a moment to organize my thoughts.**

💡 大師提點

「給我點時間想想」這句話若使用 "give me some time ...",聽起來像是需要一兩天長時間似的。如果改成 "give me a moment ..." 就能直接讓聽者明白是需要「短暫時間」來考慮。另外,面試時遇到任何問題,都會先在腦中想過一遍再回答,對吧?因此,這時用 "organize my thoughts" 最能貼切地表達「構思想法」的謹慎感。

實境對話

A: How would you explain the Internet to an alien?
B: That's an interesting question. Give a moment to organize my thoughts.
　A:你會如何跟一個外星人解釋網際網路?
　B:這問題很有趣。給我點時間想一下怎麼回答。

老外還會這樣說

❏ **Let me think about that for a second.**
　讓我想一下。

❏ **It depends. What does the alien want to do?**
　這要看情況。那個外星人想做什麼?

❏ **I'd probably just show the alien how to look that up on Wikipedia.**
　我可能會直接教外星人如何在維基百科上查資料。

🔍 關鍵字

organize [ˋɔrgə͵naɪz] (v.) 組織(想法)
look up 查詢

請問您何時會給我回覆？還是我應該主動跟您聯絡？

中式英文　When will you tell me the result? Or should I call you first?

老外這樣說　**When should I expect to hear from you? Or should I contact you?**

 大師提點

中式英文裡的 "tell me the result" 是「告知我結果」的直譯，聽起來相當呆板且有些失禮，應避免。至於想確認後續聯繫方式，精簡地說 "Should I contact you?" 即可將電話、簡訊、電子郵件等管道通通含括在內，而不僅僅是限定打電話。

 實境對話

A: Thank you very much for coming in today.
B: I enjoyed it. When should I expect to hear from you? Or should I contact you?

　A：謝謝你今天過來一趟。
　B：能跟您面談我非常高興。請問您何時會給我回覆？還是我應該主動跟您聯絡？

🧑‍💼 老外還會這樣説

❏ Thank you very much for your time. I hope to hear some good news from you soon.
非常感謝您的時間。我希望很快能接到您的好消息。

❏ Thank you. If I don't hear from you by Friday, is it OK if I give you a call?
謝謝您。如果我星期五之前還沒接到您的回覆，可以直接打電話給您嗎？

🔍 關鍵字

hear from 從……得到消息
contact [`kɑntækt] (v.) 聯絡

Unit 7

談判協商

Negotiations

讓我們先確認協商的順序。您認為如何？

🎵 **Track 089**

中式英文 Let's check the order of the negotiation first. What do you say?

老外這樣說 **Let's first agree on a procedure for the negotiation. How does that sound?**

 大師提點

在談判協商開始之前，雙方須先協調討論議題的順序，此時便可使用 "procedure" 來帶出「步驟」這項重點，以取代直譯的 "order" 一字。另外，"How does that sound?" 是老外在徵詢他人意見時經常使用的口語，各位也不妨記下來。

 實境對話

A: Let's first agree on a procedure for the negotiation. How does that sound?

B: Sure. What do you have in mind?

A：我們先確認一下協商的順序吧。您覺得如何？

B：當然。你有什麼想法？

📢 **老外還會這樣說**

❏ **I'd like to clarify a couple of procedural issues first.**
我想先釐清幾項程序上的問題。

❏ **There are a few things we should make clear before we start.**
我們應該先弄清楚幾件事然後再開始。

❏ **Before we get started, I'd like to make a few suggestions about how to proceed.**
在我們開始之前，我想針對如何進行協商提些建議。

🔍 **關鍵字**

agree on 在……上達成協議
procedure [prə`sidʒɚ] (n.) 程序；步驟
negotiation [nɪˌgoʃɪ`eʃən] (n.) 談判；協商
have in mind 想到；想要

既然我們今天的議程很緊湊，那我們是不是
應該馬上開始討論？

中式英文 Our schedule is tight today, so should we begin to discuss right now?

老外這樣說 **Since we've got a full agenda today, should we get started now?**

大師提點

凡是討論、會議的「議程」，以 "agenda" 一字表示是最貼切的，而 "full agenda"（滿滿的議程）則讓聽者有緊湊的感覺。另外，"begin to discuss" 是「開始討論」的直譯，在口語上老外並不會這麼說，因此應避免。

實境對話

A: Since we've got a full agenda today, should we get started now?
B: Sure. We're ready.

　A：既然我們今天的議程很緊湊，那我們是不是應該馬上開始討論？
　B：當然，我們都準備好了。

老外還會這樣說

❏ We have a lot to cover today, so let's get started.
今天我們有很多事項要討論，所以我們就開始吧。

❏ We have quite a few things to get through today, so let's just get right into it.
今天我們有不少事情要討論，所以我們就直接開始吧。

🔍 關鍵字

agenda [əˋdʒɛndə] (n.) 議程　　　　　**get through** 辦完（在此指討論完）

⚠ 職場成功 Tips

美國人討論事情時通常習慣 "get right to the point"（直接講正事），並避免 "beat around the bush"（顧左右而言他）。筆者前任美國老闆的口頭禪之一便是 "Stop beating around the bush and answer my question."（不要扯些有的沒的，直接回答我的問題。）

如果貴公司能保證訂購五千組，我們願意提供八五折優惠。

🎵 **Track 091**

中式英文 ┃ If you promise that you will buy 5,000 units, we will give you 15% discount.

老外這樣說 ┃ **We'd be willing to offer a 15% discount on the condition that your company guaranteed an order of 5,000 units.**

 大師提點

要提出條件和廠商討價還價，以 "We'd be willing to [do something] on the condition that your company [do something]." 此句型，即可傳達「若貴公司願意 [做某事]，我們就願意 [做某事]」之意，聽起來既專業又不會像中式英文句那樣生澀。

 實境對話

A: What's your discount on orders of this size?

B: We'd be willing to offer a 15% discount on the condition that your company guaranteed an order of 5,000 units.

A：針對這種規模的訂單，你們的優惠為何？
B：如果貴公司能保證訂購五千組，我們願意提供八五折優惠。

📢 **老外還會這樣說**

❏ **On orders of 5,000 units or more, we can offer 15%.**
訂購數量達五千組以上的話，我們可以提供八五折的優惠。

❏ **For an order of 5,000 units, we could probably knock 15% off the total.**
針對五千套的訂單，我們應該能減免全額百分之十五的貨款。

🔍 **關鍵字**

unit [ˋjunɪt] (n.) 一組；一套　　　　**knock off**（價格）減去；下跌

⚠️ **職場成功 Tips**

以下再補充兩個談判協商的好用句型：

- We can agree to ... as long as you guarantee ...（只要你們保證……我們就同意……）
- We might consider ... if you can ...（如果你們可以……我們就考慮……）

🔘 **Track 092**

中式英文 | Probably I don't have the right to decide that kind of thing.
老外這樣說 | **I'm afraid I don't have the authority to approve something like that.**

⚡ 大師提點

中式英文裡的 "right" 是「權力」之意，但是此處所討論的「權限」是針對能否決定事情而言，因此使用 "authority" 一字較貼近語意。

實境對話

A: Why don't we consider a profit-sharing model?
B: I'm afraid I don't have the authority to approve something like that.

A：我們何不考慮走分紅模式？
B：我恐怕沒有這個權限做那種決策。

老外還會這樣說

❏ **I'd have to run something like that by our board first.**
那種事情我必須先呈報給我們的董事會才行。

❏ **I'd need authorization from the owner before even discussing that.**
我需要所有人賦予的權限，才能開始討論那件事。

Unit
7

🔍 關鍵字

profit-sharing [ˋprɑfɪtˋʃɛrɪŋ] (*adj.*) 利益共享的
approve [əˋpruv] (*v.*) 批准；同意

authority [əˋθɔrətɪ] (*n.*) 職權
board [bord] (*n.*) 董事會

⚠ 職場成功 Tips

若是代表公司去談判，而自己也不是真正的 decision maker（決策者），通常不會在當下承諾任何事情。像這種情況，你可以說："I'd like to consult with my colleagues before committing to anything."（在做任何承諾之前，我想先跟同事討論一下。）

115

我認為我們雙方都要做些讓步。

🎧 **Track 093**

| 中式英文 | I think both of us need to step back a little. |

老外這樣說 **I think we both need to give a little ground here.**

💡 大師提點

"Step back a little" 聽起來像是叫人「往後退」。要表示「讓步」之意，可使用片語 "give ground" 來傳達 "concede"（退讓）的感覺。另外，"find a happy medium" 是「找出折衷辦法」的意思，也可應用於此情境。

實境對話

A: It seems that we're at an impasse.
B: I think we both need to give a little ground here.

A：看來我們陷入僵局了。
B：我想我們雙方都必須稍微各退一步才行。

老外還會這樣說

❏ I think we can both be a little more flexible here.
我認為我們都可以再稍微有彈性一點。

❏ I'm sure that if we keep at this, we'll find some common ground soon.
我相信如果我們再繼續努力，很快就能找到彼此都滿意的辦法。

❏ Let's leave this undecided for now and move on.
這件事我們現在不用做決定，先討論下個議題吧。

❏ Let's agree to disagree about this for now.
我們現在都先保留各自不同的意見吧。

🔍 關鍵字

impasse [ˋɪmpæs] (n.) 死路；僵局
flexible [ˋflɛksəbl] (adj.) 有彈性的
common ground 共通點

give ground 讓步
keep at 繼續做
agree to disagree 容許歧見

為了讓您放心，我們保證三天後會到貨。

中式英文 | In order not to let you worry, we promise you to deliver in three days.

老外這樣說 | **Don't worry about that. We guarantee three-day delivery.**

💡 大師提點

「請放心」若以 "not to let you worry" 來傳達，顯得冗長又不自然，直接說 "Don't worry about that." 即可。另外，要表示「保證」的意思，"promise" 雖然也翻譯為「承諾」，但是 "guarantee" 更能加強語氣進而帶出「保障」的意味。

實境對話

A: We're moving to a zero inventory system, so any production or shipping delays would be very costly.

B: Don't worry about that. We guarantee three-day delivery.

A：我們正在轉換成零盤存系統，所以任何生產或出貨上的延遲，都會對我們造成非常大的損失。

B：您放心，我們保證三天後將貨品送達。

老外還會這樣說

❑ That's no problem. We always deliver within 72 hours of receiving an order.

沒問題。我們收到訂單後一定會在七十二小時內出貨。

❑ I understand your concern. I can assure you that it won't be a problem.

我瞭解您的疑慮。我可以向您保證那不會是問題。

🔍 關鍵字

inventory [ˈɪnvənˌtorɪ] (n.) 庫存
guarantee [ˌgærənˈti] (v.) 保證；保障

costly [ˈkɔstlɪ] (adj.) 昂貴的；代價高的
assure [əˈʃʊr] (v.) 保證；使放心

暫停一下吧。說不定稍後可以發想出新點子。

🎧 **Track 095**

中式英文　Let's stop first. Maybe we can think of some new ideas later.

老外這樣說　**Let's take a break and hopefully we can come back with some fresh ideas.**

 大師提點

開會時難免遇到腸枯思竭的困境，要先跳過某議題，只要說 "Let's take a break." 便能表達「暫停 / 休息」之意。其後接上的 "come back with fresh ideas" 則蘊含「休息後再回來思路會更清晰」的語感。

 實境對話

A: **We can't move forward until the payment schedule is set.**
B: **Let's take a break and hopefully we can come back with some fresh ideas.**
　A：如果付款時程不先訂下來，我們就沒辦法繼續討論後續事項。
　B：先休息一下吧。或許稍後回來我們會有一些新的想法。

📢 **老外還會這樣説**

❏ **Let's take a break for lunch and see if we can come back with a few new alternatives.**
　我們先暫停去吃個午餐，看看回來之後能不能有一些其他的辦法。

❏ **Let's take a short break to give us time to talk among ourselves.**
　我們稍作休息，讓大家有時間各自討論一下。

🔍 **關鍵字**

payment [ˋpemənt] (n.) 付款　　　　　　**alternative** [ɔlˋtɜnətɪv] (n.) 供選擇的辦法

⚠ **職場成功 Tips**

談判時偶爾會遇到雙方僵持不下的狀況，此時你可以說：
- We're going round in circles. 我們在繞圈子。
- We're getting bogged down. 我們陷入僵局。

🎧 **Track 096**

中式英文 | I think all details of the contract are set down.

老外這樣說 | **I think that ties up all the loose ends with the contract.**

 大師提點

「處理事情到某一個段落」在中文裡有「搞定／收尾」的說法，而在英文裡最貼切的就是片語 "tie up loose ends"。其中 "loose ends" 意指「未了結的零星問題」。各位想像一下，把這些問題都 "tie up"（繫緊）起來，不就有「收尾」的意思了嗎？另外，中式英文裡的 "set down" 其實是指「放下／記下」之意，並不適用於此情境。

 實境對話

A: I think that ties up all the loose ends with the contract.

B: Finally!

A：我想合約中所有末了結的問題都解決了。

B：終於啊！

🔊 **老外還會這樣說**

❑ **I think that about does it for the contract. Any final concerns?**
我想合約應該沒問題了。還有什麼最後的疑慮嗎？

❑ **It's good to finally have the contract out of the way.**
太好了，終於把合約的事情搞定了。

❑ **Unless anyone has something to add, the contract is settled.**
除非還有人要補充，要不然合約就這樣定下了。

Unit
7

🔍 **關鍵字**

tie up loose ends 將細節部分搞定，做收尾的動作。

That does it. 夠了；搞定

have something out of the way 把某事搞定

settle [`sɛtl̩] (v.) 確定；決定

Track 097

中式英文　Let's react based on what will happen.

老外這樣說　**We'll have to play it by ear.**

 大師提點

協商時可能會有等對方出招再「見機行事」的情況，此時就可以使用最貼切的片語 "play it by ear" 來表達。順帶一提，英文還有 "play by ear" 的說法，意思是「靠（聽過的）記憶彈奏樂器」。

實境對話

A: **How is the new law going to affect us?**

B: **It's hard to say. We'll have to play it by ear.**

　A：那條新法令將會對我們產生什麼影響？

　B：很難說，我們只能見機行事。

老外還會這樣說

❑ **We'll just have to wait and see.**
　我們只得靜觀其變了。

❑ **Let's cross that bridge when we come to it.**
　我們先看事情如何演變再說吧。（船到橋頭自然直。）

❑ **Let's just take each day as it comes.**
　我們走一步算一步吧。

 關鍵字

affect [əˋfɛkt] (v.) 影響

120

我們需要試著跳脫框架來看此事。

🎧 Track 098

中式英文 We need to try to see this thing without frames.

老外這樣說 **We have to try to think outside the box on this.**

⚡ 大師提點

中文的「跳脫框架思考」一詞在英文裡是 "think outside the box"，也就是「不要被舊思維限制住」的意思。至於中式英文裡的 "see things without frames"，老外並沒有這樣的說法。

實境對話

A: The exclusivity clause is a real sticking point.

B: We have to try to think outside the box on this.

　　A：獨家經營權條款是真正的癥結點。

　　B：我們得試著從別的角度去思考一下。

📢 老外還會這樣說

❏ **Let's not get hung up on this one issue.**
我們別在這問題上鑽牛角尖。

❏ **I'm confident we can come up with some creative solutions.**
我相信我們一定能想到有創意的解決辦法。

❏ **We shouldn't let this one little detail threaten the whole deal.**
我們不應該讓這個小細節影響到整個案子。

Unit
7

🔍 關鍵字

exclusivity [ɛksklu`sɪvətɪ] (n.) 獨有；獨家（經營、代理）

clause [klɔz] (n.) 條款

sticking point 癥結點

think outside the box 跳脫框架思考

hung up on something 被某事拖累住

come up with 想出

我們看看有沒有折衷的辦法吧。

 Track 099

中式英文 Let's find a way good for both of us.

老外這樣說 **Let's try to meet halfway on that.**

 大師提點

談判協商時，若遇到對方提出對我方不利的要求而要表達異議時，美國人通常會先緩和地以 "I see what you mean, but ..." 做開場白，接著尋求對雙方有利的折衷辦法，而不會貿然地就說「我不同意」。

實境對話

A: We're prepared to pay in full after receiving the final shipment.
B: Hmm. Let's try to meet halfway on that.

　　A：我們準備在收到最後一批貨品後支付全額的款項。
　　B：嗯，我們看看有沒有折衷的辦法吧。

 老外還會這樣說

❏ **Well, that would be one way to do it. Usually we …**
　嗯，那的確是一種進行的方法。通常我們……

❏ **We usually require payment before then, but we have some flexibility there.**
　我們通常要求事先付款，但還是有討論的空間。

🔍 **關鍵字**

in full 全額
meet halfway 折衷
flexibility [ˌflɛksəˈbɪlətɪ] (n.) 彈性

看來我們在交貨期這方面無法達成共識。

🔊 Track 100

中式英文　It seems that we can't agree with each other on the delivery date.

老外這樣說　**The delivery date really seems to be what's holding us back.**

💡 大師提點

片語 "hold back" 有 "to keep from moving"、也就是「牽制」的感覺，用在本句情境中即可解釋為雙方沒有共識。中式英文裡所使用的 "we can't agree with each other" 是「雙方不同意彼此」的直譯，並無法靈活地傳達出停滯於某點的意涵。

實境對話

A: I really want to wrap this thing up.
B: Well, the delivery date really seems to be what's holding us back.
　A：我真的很想把這件事情搞定。
　B：嗯，看來交貨日期就是導致我們無法取得共識的原因。

老外還會這樣說

❑ **The only thing that isn't resolved is the delivery date.**
唯一還沒解決的問題就是交貨期。

❑ **The delivery date is the only outstanding issue.**
只剩下交貨期還沒談出結果。

❑ **We'll be done as soon as we nail down the delivery date.**
一旦我們敲定出貨日就算大功告成了。

Unit
7

🔍 關鍵字

wrap up 完成；總結
delivery date 交貨日期
hold back 保留；阻礙
outstanding [`aut`stændɪŋ] (adj.) 未解決的；未償付的
nail down 敲定

Unit 8

★ ★ ★ ★ ★ ★ ★ ★ ★ ★ ★ ★ ★ ★ ★ ★ ★ ★ ★

客戶應對

Interacting with Customers

100 我想表達 **您對我們的哪一項產品最有興趣？**

  Track 101

中式英文　Which product do you want to purchase?

老外這樣說　**Which of our products are you most interested in?**

🔅 大師提點

詢問客戶對什麼產品有興趣，最直接的說法便是使用 "be interested in" 這個片語。通常比較不會預期客戶洽詢完立即下訂單，因此有經驗的業務不會開門見山地問 "What do you want to purchase?"（你想買什麼？）

👓 實境對話

A: Which of our products are you most interested in?
B: I've mostly been looking at your Extreme 1 line.

A：您對我們的哪一項產品最有興趣？
B：我一直很注意你們的 Extreme 1 系列。

📢 老外還會這樣説

❑ **What is it that you want to use our products to do?**
您想要將我們的產品應用在何種用途上？

❑ **What are you in the market for?**
您想要找的是什麼樣的產品？

❑ **Are you looking for a high-performance model?**
您是否在找高效能的型號？

❑ **If you're on a tight budget, you might consider the ES600.**
如果您的預算有限，可以考慮 ES600 看看。

🔍 關鍵字

high-performance [`haɪ pɚ`fɔrməns] (adj.) 高效能的
model [`madl] (n.) 型號；模式
on a tight budget 預算有限
consider [kən`sɪdɚ] (v.) 考慮；認為

就品質而言，我們的產品是業界第一。

🎵 Track 102

中式英文　Speaking of quality, our products are number one in the field.

老外這樣說　**In terms of quality, our products are second to none.**

 大師提點

事實上，"speaking of [something]" 這個片語帶有些許「轉移話題」的感覺。例如，
"Cathy's on vacation. Speaking of vacation, I'll go to Thailand next month."（凱西去
度假了。對了，提到度假，我下個月要去泰國。）本來在討論凱西的事，後來轉移話
題到自己身上。另外，「第一名」若說 "number one" 老外也聽得懂，但是使用
"second to none" 更顯道地，表示 "better than anything else"（比其他的更好）。

🗨 **實境對話**

A: That's a little more than we're accustomed to paying.

B: Perhaps. But in terms of quality, our products are second to none.

　　A：這和我們通常的買價相比，稍微高了點。

　　B：也許是這樣沒錯。但是就品質而言，我們的產品是業界第一。

 老外還會這樣說

❏ **You get what you pay for.**

　一分錢一分貨。

❏ **Well, you do have to pay a little more for this level of quality.**

　嗯，您若想要這個等級的品質，就必須多付一點錢。

❏ **I'm sure that you'll quickly come to appreciate the quality of our products.**

　我相信您很快就能體會我們產品的高品質了。

Unit
8

🔍 **關鍵字**

accustomed [əˋkʌstəmd] (*adj.*) 習慣的；通常的
in terms of 就……而言
second to none 不亞於任何人（比其他人都還要棒）
appreciate [əˋpriʃɪˏet] (*v.*) 欣賞；感激；體會

如果我們訂購超過一千組，你可以給我們什麼樣的折扣？

Track 103

中式英文 If we order 1,000 and above units, what discount will you give us?

老外這樣說 **If we buy more than 1,000 units, what kind of discount can you offer us?**

大師提點

「超過 [某數量]」應以 "more than [amount]" 來表示，"[amount] and above" 是不正確的。另外，「打折」的說法是 "offer ... discount"（提供折扣），而非直接中譯成 "give ... discount"（給折扣）。

實境對話

A: **If we buy more than 1,000 units, what kind of discount can you offer us?**

B: **We offer 5% on purchases of 3,000 units or more.**

　A：如果我們購買超過一千組，你可以提供什麼樣的折扣給我們？

　B：我們提供購買三千組以上打九五折的優惠。

老外還會這樣說

❏ **Is that the best price you can offer?**
那是你所能提供的最低價格嗎？

❏ **Would you take $29,000 if we agreed to purchase more than 1,000 units?**
如果我們同意購買超過一千組，能算兩萬九嗎？

❏ **I'm afraid we just can't go that high.**
我們恐怕無法接受那麼高的價格。

關鍵字

purchase [ˋpɝtʃəs] (n.) 購買

我來電是想詢問一筆尚未結清的款項。

🎧 Track 104

中式英文 I'm calling to ask why you haven't paid for an order.

老外這樣說 **I'm calling about an unpaid invoice.**

 大師提點

要表達「尚未付清」，可使用形容詞 "unpaid" 這個字，也就是 "not yet paid" 的意思。至於，中式英文例句中的 "why you haven't paid ..."，老外並不會這樣說。

 實境對話

A: **I'm calling about an unpaid invoice.**
B: **I'm sorry. I think you have the wrong number.**
　A：我打電話來是要確認一筆尚未結清的款項。
　B：抱歉，我想你打錯電話了。

📢 **老外還會這樣說**

❏ **I'm calling about an outstanding invoice. When can we expect payment?**
我來電是想詢問有關未結清出貨單的事。請問我們何時能收到款項？

❏ **I'm calling about an overdue invoice. Can we expect payment this week?**
我來電是想詢問有關逾期請款單的事。請問我們這週是否能收到帳款？

❏ **I'm calling about an invoice that was due on May 15.**
我來電是想確認一張五月十五日到期的發票。

❏ **I'm calling about an invoice that's currently 45 days past due.**
我來電是想確認一張款項已經逾期四十五天的帳單。

Unit 8

🔍 **關鍵字**

invoice [ˋɪnvɔɪs] (n.) 發票；出貨單；請款單
overdue [ˋovɚˋdju] (adj.) 未兌的；過期的
currently [ˋkɝəntlɪ] (adv.) 目前；現在
have the wrong number 打錯電話
due [dju] (adj.) 到期的；應支付的
past due 過期

根據合約，款項必須在三十天內付清。

🎵 **Track 105**

中式英文 According to the contract, you must pay within a month.

老外這樣說 **According to the contract, payment must be made within thirty days.**

💡 大師提點

地產大亨 Donald Trump（唐納・川普）常說 "It's nothing personal. It's all about business."（無關個人，公事公辦。），和廠商、客戶催收帳款也不例外。中式英文的說法 "You must pay ..." 聽起來好像是針對個人；若主詞換一下，改說 "Payment must be made ..." 語氣一轉就變成是針對 "payment"「款項」這件事，聽起來便是對事不對人了。

實境對話

A: We would really prefer to make quarterly payments.

B: I understand, but according to the contract, payment must be made within thirty days.

A：我們很希望能夠以分季的方式付款。

B：我瞭解，但是根據合約，款項必須在三十天之內付清。

老外還會這樣說

❏ **Payment must be made within thirty days, in accordance with the contract.**

根據合約，款項必須在三十天內付清。

❏ **The contract states that shipment won't be made until the initial payment has been received.**

依照合約規定，我們收到訂金後才會出貨。

🔍 關鍵字

make payment 付款

shipment [ˈʃɪpmənt] (*n.*) 出貨

in accordance with 依照；與……一致

initial payment 首期付款；訂金

我不需要知道確切的數字。只要大概就好。

中式英文 I don't need to know a specific number. Just give me a general number.

老外這樣說 **I don't need an exact number. A ballpark figure would be fine.**

大師提點

提到「大約」，許多人腦中會浮現 "about, around, approximate" 這幾個字，但是在口語中有一個更道地的表達方式——"a ballpark number" 或 "a ballpark figure"。"ballpark" 原指「棒球場」，場地很大但是又在一定範圍內，因而衍生出 "a ballpark figure"「大概抓一個數字」的意思。

實境對話

A: **I don't need an exact number. A ballpark figure would be fine.**
B: **Off the top of my head, I'd say that would run about NT$290 or NT$300 per piece.**
　A：我不需要確切的數字。只要一個大概的數目就可以。
　B：要我現在直接講的話，每件約新台幣兩百九或三百元左右。

老外還會這樣說

❑ **Can you give me a rough idea of how much all this is going to cost?**
你能不能大概告訴我這些東西全部要花多少錢？

❑ **How much do you usually get for these?**
你們這些東西的價格通常是多少？

❑ **Could you do a quick back-of-the-envelope calculation now? I want to have a better idea of what you charge.**
你能不能現在很快地大概算一下？我想瞭解一下你們怎麼收費。

🔍 關鍵字

ballpark figure 大概估計
rough [rʌf] (*adj.*) 粗估的

off the top of one's head 未經仔細考慮或計算
back-of-the-envelope 概略的

交貨作業時間也是我們必須考慮的因素。

🔊 Track 107

中式英文　The shipping duration is one of our concerns.

老外這樣說　**Lead time is also something we need to take into account.**

 大師提點

業界的慣用語 "lead time" 是指「下訂單之後到交貨的所需時間」，英文裡並沒有 "shipping duration" 的說法。另外，「將 [某事] 考慮進去」可以用片語 "take [something] into account" 或 "take [something] into consideration" 來表達。

 實境對話

A: Is there anything else we haven't discussed?
B: Lead time is also something we need to take into account.

　A：還有沒有我們沒討論到的事項？
　B：我們也需要考慮一下交貨作業時間的問題。

🔊 老外還會這樣説

❑ **What we really need to do is reduce our lead time. Six weeks is ridiculous.**
我們的當務之急是縮短交貨作業時間。六週實在是太離譜了。

❑ **If you can't manage a shorter lead time, you'll have to maintain a larger inventory.**
如果你們沒辦法縮短交貨作業時間，就必須要有更多的庫存才行。

🔍 關鍵字

lead time 訂貨至交貨的時間
manage [ˋmænɪdʒ] (v.) 設法；管理

reduce [rɪˋdjus] (v.) 減少；降低
maintain [menˋten] (v.) 維持

⚠ 職場成功 Tips

關於出貨，"shipping" 和 "handling" 有何差別？ "shipping" 顧名思義就是「運送」，而 "handling" 則包括 "packing"「包裝」等處理的部分。

運送時程視您的位置而定，但通常我們會在七個工作天內送達。

🎧 **Track 108**

中式英文 The delivery schedule depends on your position, but we usually ship within seven days.

老外這樣說 **Delivery time varies depending on location, but we usually deliver within seven business days.**

💡 大師提點

此例句提到的「位置」，應使用 "location"「地點」一字，而非 "position"「方位」。
另外，「送達（到貨）」應以 "deliver" 表達，"ship" 指的是「出貨」。

 實境對話

A: How long will it take to receive our order?
B: Delivery time varies depending on location, but we usually deliver within seven business days.

A：要多久才能收到我們訂的貨品？
B：運送時程依您的所在地而有所不同，但我們通常會在七個工作天內將貨品送達。

 老外還會這樣說

❏ **If you're in a hurry, you're welcome to pick your order up at our warehouse anytime.**
如果您很急的話，歡迎隨時到我們的倉庫提領您所訂的貨品。

❏ **For an extra fee we can guarantee next-day delivery on orders received before 3:00 p.m.**
只要支付額外的費用，我們就能保證在隔天下午三點前將貨品送達。

❏ **If we have it in stock, we can usually deliver within 48 hours.**
如果我們有庫存的話，通常在四十八小時內就能到貨。

Unit
8

🔍 關鍵字

warehouse [ˋwɛrˌhaʊs] (*n.*) 倉庫
fee [fi] (*n.*) 費用

extra [ˋɛkstrə] (*adj.*) 額外的
stock [stɑk] (*n.*) 庫存

那些要求對我們來說太超過了。

🔘 Track 109

| 中式英文 | Those requirements are too over for us. |

| 老外這樣說 | **I'm afraid we can't accept those terms.** |

 大師提點

「太超過」要怎麼說？ "Those requirements are too over ..." 顯然是直譯下的說法。事實上，像這種情況，老外通常會婉轉地用 "We can't accept ..." 來表達對過份要求無法接受之意。另外，此處所謂的「要求」指的應是對方所開出的「條件」，因此使用 "terms" 這個字才正確。

 實境對話

A: **We'll need to receive the order within 14 days of placing it, and we won't be able to pay for shipping.**

B: **I'm afraid we can't accept those terms.**

A：我們需要在下訂後十四天之內收到貨品，而且我們無法支付運費。

B：這樣的條件我們恐怕無法接受。

 老外還會這樣説

❏ **We can't agree to those terms.**
我們無法同意那些條件。

❏ **Those terms are a little too restrictive for us.**
那些條件對我們而言有點太嚴苛了。

❏ **We'd be willing to accept that if you could extend the lead time to 21 days.**
如果您可以將交貨作業時間延長至二十一天，我們就願意接受。

❏ **If you're willing to pay the full amount up front, we could do that.**
如果您願意預先付清款項，我們就同意這麼做。

🔍 **關鍵字**

term [tɜm] (*n.*) 條件；條款　　　　**restrictive** [rɪ`strɪktɪv] (*adj.*) 約束的；限制的

🔊 **Track 110**

中式英文 Almost all of our customers are very satisfied.

老外這樣說 **We have one of the highest customer service ratings in the industry.**

 大師提點

中式英文例句提到 "… our customers are very satisfied." (我們的客戶非常滿意。)，此說法過於籠統，而且聽起來不專業。因此，若改成："We have … highest customer service rating in the industry." 便能帶出「我們擁有業界最高的客戶滿意度」之意。

 實境對話

A: **What happens when something goes wrong?**

B: **We'll take care of it. We have one of the highest customer service ratings in the industry.**

A：如果發生問題該怎麼辦？

B：我們會處理的。我們是擁有業界最高客服評價的公司之一。

📣 **老外還會這樣説**

❏ **We have a 98% customer satisfaction rating.**
我們的客戶滿意度高達百分之九十八。

❏ **Customer satisfaction is our primary goal.**
讓客戶滿意是我們的首要目標。

❏ **We aim for 100% customer satisfaction.**
我們的目標是百分之百的客戶滿意度。

Unit 8

🔍 **關鍵字**

go wrong 失敗；出問題
industry [ˋɪndəstrɪ] (n.) 工業；產業
goal [gol] (n.) 目標

rating [ˋretɪŋ] (n.) 等級；評價
primary [ˋpraɪˏmərɪ] (adj.) 主要的；首要的
aim for 致力於；以……為目標

Unit 9

宴會用餐

Events

我今天不太想吃中式餐點耶！

Track 111

中式英文 Today I don't really want to eat Chinese food.

老外這樣說 **I'm not really in the mood for Chinese today.**

 大師提點

中式英文句裡的 "don't want to + do [something]" 雖說也是「不想做 [某事]」之意，且老外一樣聽得懂，但是稍嫌呆板。而使用片語 "not in the mood for [something]" 能傳達出「不想 / 沒那個心情」的感覺，相對之下更加道地、自然。

 實境對話

A: Do you feel like going to Szechwan Palace again?
B: I'm not really in the mood for Chinese today.

A：你想不想再去「四川皇宮」餐廳一次？
B：我今天不太想吃中國菜欸。

老外還會這樣説

❏ **I'm sick of Kung Pao Chicken.**
宮保雞丁我已經吃到膩了。

❏ **I could go for some Mexican.**
去吃墨西哥菜也不錯。

❏ **Anything but noodles.**
只要不是吃麵就好。

❏ **I feel like something light.**
我想吃點清淡的料理。

關鍵字

feel like 想要 　　　　　　**in the mood for** 有心情做某事 　　　　　　**sick of** 厭倦

⚠ 職場成功 Tips

上述 "in the mood for" 片語還可有些變化。例如，"in a good mood" 指「心情愉悅」，"in a bad mood" 是「心情不佳」的意思。平時在公司你可能會說："I got a big order, so I'm in a really good mood today."（我得到一筆大訂單，所以我今天心情超好。）

Track 112

中式英文 | What's your recommendation?

老外這樣說 | **What do you recommend?**

大師提點

老外偏好使用 "power verbs"（強而有力的動詞）以顯示 "action"（行動力）。此處的 "recommendation"（推薦）一字，其本身有動詞形式 "recommend" 可使用，因此 "What do you recommend?" 會比較精簡有力。或是說 "Could you recommend something special?"（你可以推薦一些特別的嗎？）也沒問題。

實境對話

A: Are you ready to order?
B: What do you recommend?

A：您準備好要點餐了嗎？

B：你推薦什麼菜色？

 老外還會這樣說

❏ **Are there any local specialties that you'd suggest?**

你們這裡有什麼道地的餐點可以推薦一下嗎？

❏ **Do you have something that's not too oily?**

你們有沒有比較不油膩的料理？

❏ **What do you have that's kind of light?**

你們有什麼菜是比較清淡的嗎？

Unit
9

⚠ **職場成功 Tips**

上述提到的 "power verbs" 非常適合在商務環境使用。請再比較以下例子，便可看出 "power verbs" 更具顯示行動力的功能。

（弱）He makes a suggestion ...　　（強）He suggests ...

（弱）He put forward a proposal ...　　（強）He proposed that ...

（弱）She gave me encouragement ...　　（強）She encouraged me to ...

你們有素食嗎？

Track 113

中式英文　Do you sell vegetable food?

老外這樣說　**Do you have anything vegetarian?**

大師提點

「素食」的英文怎麼說？很簡單，就是 "vegetarian"。此字當名詞時，是「素食者」的意思；當形容詞時，則指「素菜的／吃素的」之意。至於 "vegetable food"，英文並沒有這個說法。

 實境對話

A: What can I get for you tonight?

B: Do you have anything vegetarian?

　　A：您今天晚上想吃什麼？

　　B：你們有素食嗎？

 老外還會這樣說

❏ **Do you have any vegetarian dishes?**
你們有沒有什麼素食料理？

❏ **Is there any meat in the tomato soup?**
番茄湯是葷的嗎？

❏ **Could you make sure there are no onions or garlic in the omelet?**
我的蛋餅裡面可不可以不要加任何洋蔥或大蒜？

❏ **Do you have any vegan desserts?**
你們有沒有純素的甜點？

🔍 關鍵字

onion [ˋʌnjən] (n.) 洋蔥

omelet [ˋɑmlɪt] (n.) 蛋餅；煎蛋捲

dessert [dɪˋzɜt] (n.) 甜點

garlic [ˋgɑrlɪk] (n.) 大蒜

vegan [ˋvɛgən] (adj.) 純素食的

※ **desert** [ˋdɛzət] (n.) 沙漠〔易混淆〕

可以續杯嗎？

中式英文 May I have one more of it for free?

老外這樣說 **Could I have a refill, please?**

 大師提點

"Fill" 指「裝滿」，那麼 "refill" 就是「再裝滿」之意，在英文中即代表「續杯」的意思。至於 "May I have one more of it for free?"，聽起來好像在強調 "for free"（免費）的感覺，但是通常所謂的「續杯」大都不再另外收費，因此不必特別強調。

 實境對話

A: Is there anything else I can get for you?
B: Yes, could I have a refill, please?

A：您還需要什麼嗎？
B：是的，麻煩可以幫我續杯嗎？

老外還會這樣說

❑ We need some more water, please.
麻煩你，我們需要多一點水。

❑ Could I get another beer, please?
麻煩可以再給我一瓶啤酒嗎？

❑ Excuse me, could I have some more tea?
不好意思，我可以再多要一點茶嗎？

❑ I'll have another latte.
我還要再一杯拿鐵。

Unit
9

關鍵字

refill [`rifɪl] (*n.*) 飲料續杯
latte [`lɑte] (*n.*) 拿鐵咖啡

不好意思。我們已經等十五分鐘了，飲料還沒送來。

Track 115

中式英文　Excuse me. We've been waiting for 15 minutes, but the drinks haven't come yet.

老外這樣說　**Excuse me. We've been waiting for 15 minutes for our drinks.**

大師提點

如何用英文「催促餐點」？ "Our drinks haven't come yet." 顯然是中文的直譯，聽在老外耳裡很奇怪。事實上，他們都會這樣說： "We've been waiting for [how long] for our meals/drinks."（我們已經等餐點 / 飲料等了 [多久] 了。）

實境對話

A: **Excuse me. We've been waiting for 15 minutes for our drinks.**
B: **I'll check on that right away.**

　　A：不好意思。我們已經等十五分鐘了，飲料還沒送來。
　　B：我馬上去幫你們確認。

老外還會這樣說

❏ **Could you check and see how our order is coming?**
　你能不能幫忙確認一下我們的餐點好了沒？

❏ **I'm sorry. This isn't what I ordered.**
　對不起，這不是我點的餐點。

❏ **It's a little cold in here. Could you turn down the air conditioning?**
　這裡面有點冷。你能不能把空調的溫度調高一點？

❏ **Would it be possible to reseat us?**
　你能幫我們換一下座位嗎？

⚠ 職場成功 Tips

中文裡常使用「請、謝謝、對不起」來讓溝通更順暢，英文也不例外。要求他人幫忙確認某事時，老外多會使用 "Excuse me, could you ... please?"、"Could I have ...?" 或 "Is it OK if you ...?" 等句型。

不好意思。這牛排太老了，我點的是三分熟。

🎵 **Track 116**

中式英文 | Excuse me. This steak is too old. I wanted it softer.

老外這樣說 | **Excuse me. This steak is overdone. I ordered rare.**

⚡ 大師提點

「牛排太老」和「幾分熟」的英文怎麼說？當然不能用中譯的方式說成 "too old" 和 "soft" 囉！老外通常會以 "overdone" 或 "overcooked" 來表示「食物煮太久（而導致口感變硬）」。另外，牛排的熟度分為 "well done"（全熟）、"medium well"（七分熟）、"medium"（五分熟）、"medium rare"（四分熟）以及 "rare"（三分熟）等。

實境對話

A: Excuse me. This steak is overdone. I ordered rare.

B: I'm sorry. Let me take that and bring you a new one.

A：不好意思。這牛排太老了，我點的是三分熟。

B：很抱歉。我馬上幫您收走，再為您送上一份新的。

📢 老外還會這樣說

❏ **I'm sorry. This chicken is undercooked.**
對不起，這份雞肉沒煮熟。

❏ **My soup is cold. Could you take it back and heat it up?**
我的湯是冷的，你能不能拿回去再將它熱一下？

❏ **I'm sorry, but this is just too spicy for me.**
對不起，這份料理對我來說太辣了。

Unit
9

🔍 關鍵字

overdone [ˋovɚˋdʌn] (*adj.*) 煮得過度的
rare [rɛr] (*adj.*) 三分熟的
undercooked [ˋʌndɚˏkʊkt] (*adj.*) 尚未煮熟的
heat up 加熱（食物）
spicy [ˋspaɪsɪ] (*adj.*) 辣的

我飽到吃不下甜點了。

中式英文 I'm too full to eat dessert.

老外這樣說 **I'm afraid I didn't save any room for dessert.**

 大師提點

中式英文句的說法應用了 "too ... to ..."（太……而無法……）這個句型，雖然沒有
錯誤，但是在口語中老外更常說 "I didn't save any room for ..."（太飽而無法再
吃……了）。這裡的 "room" 指胃裡的 "space"（空間），「胃裡沒有空間」即為「吃
不下任何東西」之意。

 實境對話

A: The cheesecake here is fantastic!
B: I'm afraid I didn't save any room for dessert.

A：這裡的起司蛋糕超好吃的！
B：我飽到肚子已經沒有空間再吃甜點了。

📢 **老外還會這樣說**

❏ **I can't eat another bite.**
我一口都吃不下了。

❏ **I'm stuffed. Maybe next time.**
我好飽。下次再吃吧。

❏ **Why don't we share a slice?**
我們要不要一起分一片吃？

❏ **Just coffee for me. You guys go ahead.**
我喝咖啡就好了。你們吃吧。

🔍 **關鍵字**

fantastic [fæn`tæstɪk] (*adj.*) 極好的；驚人的
bite [baɪt] (*n.*) 一口之量
stuffed [stʌft] (*adj.*) 吃飽了的
slice [slaɪs] (*n.*) 切片；薄片

🎧 Track 118

中式英文　Do you want to drink some wine? Give me the wine list please?

老外這樣說　**How about some wine? Could you pass me the wine list?**

⚡ 大師提點

中式英文句 "Give me the wine list …" 聽起來有命令的感覺，要請人家幫忙時，應以禮貌詢問的方式開頭。例如："Could you pass me [something]?"（你可以將 [某物] 遞給我嗎？）

 實境對話

A: We should order drinks.
B: How about some wine? Could you pass me the wine list?

A：我們應該點一些飲料。
B：你想喝點酒嗎？可以把酒單遞給我嗎？

 老外還會這樣說

❏ **Could I see the wine list, please?**
麻煩可以讓我看一下酒單嗎？

❏ **Is their house wine any good?**
他們的招牌酒好喝嗎？

❏ **Do they serve wine by the glass?**
他們有提供單杯份的酒嗎？

❏ **What do you think would go well with the steak?**
你們覺得什麼飲料搭配牛排喝最對味？

Unit
9

🔍 關鍵字

wine [waɪn] (*n.*) 酒；葡萄酒
wine list 酒類一覽表
house wine 招牌酒；特色酒
go well with 搭配得好

Track 119

中式英文　May I bring something to eat from the food table for you?

老外這樣說　**Would you like me to get you anything from the buffet?**

 大師提點

"Bring" 是「帶來」的意思，但在此處說話者要表達的是「去拿」，因此應使用 "get" 這個字。另外，可隨意拿取食物的餐台叫 "buffet"，並沒有 "food table" 這種說法。

 實境對話

A: Would you like me to get you anything from the buffet?
B: No thanks. I'm good.

　A：要我幫你從自助餐台拿點東西吃嗎？
　B：不用，謝謝。不需要。

📢 **老外還會這樣説**

❑ **Does anyone want another slice of cake?**
有人想要再吃一塊蛋糕嗎？

❑ **Could I get you another beer while I'm up?**
要不要我幫你順便拿一瓶啤酒？

❑ **Save my seat. I'll be right back with some more cookies for us.**
幫我顧一下位子。我去拿一些餅乾回來給大家吃，馬上回來。

❑ **I'm going to grab a couple more pineapple cakes for us before they're all gone.**
在鳳梨酥被搶光之前，我去拿一些回來給大家吃。

🔍 **關鍵字**

buffet [bʌˋfe] (n.) 自助餐；自助餐台
grab [græb] (v.) 取；抓
pineapple cake 鳳梨酥

我可以跟你們一起聊天嗎？

🎵 Track 120

中式英文 Can I chat with you?

老外這樣說 **Mind if I join you?**

 大師提點

提到「聊天」，很多人會立即想到 "chat" 這個字，但是在國外幾乎沒有人會說 "Can I chat with you?"！簡單地用 "Mind if I join you?" 表達最自然，其中 "join"（參加）有「融入」的感覺。

 實境對話

A: Mind if I join you?
B: Not at all. I'm Jessie, and this is Brad.

A：介意我加入你們的談話嗎？
B：一點也不會。我叫潔希，這位是布萊德。

🔊 **老外還會這樣說**

❏ **Do you mind if I sit with you?**
介意我坐你旁邊嗎？

❏ **Is this seat taken?**
這個位子有人坐嗎？

❏ **Hi. Are you guys talking about the factory in Dongguan?**
嗨，你們是不是正在聊有關東莞工廠的事？

❏ **Hello, I'm Pat. I just transferred from the head office.**
你好，我叫派特。我剛從總公司調過來。

Unit
9

🔍 **關鍵字**

head office 總公司

你們家真溫馨。

中式英文 ｜ Your house is so warm.

老外這樣說 ｜ **You have a lovely home.**

⚡ 大師提點

要如何用英文表示「溫馨的家」？很簡單，就用 "lovely home"。順帶一提，如果要讚美他人的辦公室更簡單，只要說 "You have a nice office." 就可以了。

實境對話

A: I'm so glad you could come!

B: Me too. You have a lovely home.

A：我很高興你能過來！

B：我也是。你們家真溫馨。

老外還會這樣說

❏ **I love your kitchen!**

我好喜歡你的廚房！

❏ **I don't know what you're serving, but I brought a Pinot Noir.**

我不知道你準備了什麼菜，但是我帶了一瓶黑比諾葡萄酒來。

❏ **You've got to give me the recipe for this soup.**

你一定要給我這道湯的食譜。

❏ **This pie is delicious. Did you make it from scratch?**

這派真美味。完全是你自己做的嗎？

🔍 關鍵字

serve [sɜv] (v.) 服務；上菜

have got to 一定；必須

recipe [ˋrɛsəpɪ] (n.) 食譜

from scratch 從頭開始

這太棒了！但是你真的不需要破費買東西送我。

中式英文　This is great, but there's no need to spend money buying things for me.

老外這樣說　**That's so nice! But you really didn't have to get me anything.**

大師提點

中式英文例句所提到的 "spend money buying things for me" 完全是「花錢買東西給我」的直譯，聽起來相當呆板。在英文口語中，"get [someone] [something]" 即可代表「給 [某人] 買 [某物]」之意。

實境對話

A: This is for you. It's from Delft, which is famous for its ceramics.
B: That's so nice! But you really didn't have to get me anything.

　　A：這是給你的。它來自以陶瓷出名的台夫特。
　　B：這太好了！但你實在不需要破費買東西送我。

老外還會這樣說

❏ Wow. Thank you! You didn't have to do that.
　哇，謝謝！你不需要這樣做的。

❏ Thank you. You didn't have to go to so much trouble.
　謝謝你。你不需要這麼麻煩。

❏ Oh, that's lovely. I love ceramics! Thank you.
　噢，真漂亮。我很喜歡陶瓷器！謝謝你。

❏ Thank you. This really means a lot to me.
　謝謝你。這對我來說意義重大。

Unit 9

🔍 關鍵字

ceramics [sə`ræmɪks] (*n.*) 陶瓷

你能來真好！

中式英文　Your arrival is really good.

老外這樣說　**It was good to have you over.**

 大師提點

此句是做東的主人感謝賓客出席所說的話。雖然 "arrival" 是「來到」的意思，但是直譯成 "Your arrival is good." 可能第一時間老外會一頭霧水。像這種情境，老外通常會使用 "have you over" 這個片語，其中表達了 "come and visit us"（來看我們）的涵義。

 實境對話

A: It was good to have you over.
B: Well, thanks for having me.

　A：你能來真好！
　B：嗯，謝謝你邀請我來。

🗣 **老外還會這樣説**

❏ **Well, you've got a big day tomorrow. I don't want to keep you.**
　嗯，你明天還要忙，我就不留你了。

❏ **We'll have to do this more often.**
　我們以後要經常這樣聚聚。

❏ **Would you like to take some cake home?**
　你要不要帶一些蛋糕回家？

❏ **I hope you don't mind, but I've packed a few cookies for you to take with you.**
　我裝了一些餅乾讓你帶回去，希望你不會介意。

🔍 **關鍵字**

have someone over　邀請某人到家裡
pack [pæk] (v.) 包裝；打包

Track 124

中式英文 Thank you for inviting me and I enjoyed that.

老外這樣說 **Thank you for a wonderful evening.**

 大師提點

此句為宴會之後的感謝語。中式英文例句裡的 "Thank you for inviting me." 問題不大，但是其後的 "I enjoyed that." 就不知所云了。老外通常會簡單地以 "Thank you for a wonderful evening." 來表達「感謝對方款待」之意。

實境對話

A: Thank you so much for coming.
B: Thank you for a wonderful evening.

A：非常謝謝你們能來。
B：謝謝您的盛情款待。

 老外還會這樣說

❏ **Thank you so much. Everything was delicious.**
謝謝你。每一樣東西都很好吃。

❏ **I really enjoyed myself tonight.**
我今天晚上過得非常愉快。

❏ **We'll have to get together at my place next time.**
下次我們得改到我家聚一聚。

❏ **Well, it's getting late. We should be heading back soon.**
嗯，有點晚了。我們差不多該回家了。

Unit
9

關鍵字

enjoy oneself 過得愉快；玩得盡興

⚠ 職場成功 Tips

商務場合除了上班時間談公事，下班後邀請外國客戶或合作夥伴到家裡作客也是常有的事。但記得，若有機會受到外國人的款待，別忘了在事後寄封 email 或訊息給對方以表達感謝。

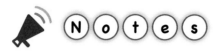

Unit 10

展覽諮詢

Trade Shows

明天就要參展了，可是印刷廠還沒把我們的文宣品印好！

🎵 Track 125

中式英文　We're going to join in the exhibition, but the print factory hasn't finished printing our DM.

老外這樣說　**The exhibition starts tomorrow and the printer hasn't finished printing our sales materials yet.**

💡 大師提點

「明天就要參展」以 "exhibition" 為主詞，說成 "The exhibition starts tomorrow." 可避免每次都以「你、我、他」等當主詞開頭。另外，宣傳用的文宣用 "DM" (Direct Mailing) 表示略顯狹隘，因為文宣可能還包括 brochure（手冊）、flyer（傳單）、pamphlet（小冊子）等，而若使用 "sales materials"（行銷文宣資料）一詞則可含括各類的文宣品。

🗣 實境對話

A: What's wrong?
B: The exhibition starts tomorrow and the printer hasn't finished printing our sales materials yet.

A：怎麼了嗎？
B：展覽明天就要開幕了，但是印刷廠還沒把我們的行銷文宣印完。

📣 老外還會這樣說

❑ **The space we've been assigned doesn't match the online description.**
我們被分配到的空間和網路上描述的不一樣。

❑ **We're going to need two additional tables and four more chairs.**
我們還需要兩張桌子和四張椅子。

❑ **We've already lost our Internet connection several times today.**
今天我們的網路已經中斷好幾次了。

🔍 關鍵字

exhibition [ˌɛksəˈbɪʃən] (n.) 展覽；展示會
assign [əˈsaɪn] (v.) 指定；分派

printer [ˈprɪntə] (n.) 印刷業者；印表機
additional [əˈdɪʃənl] (adj.) 額外的；另外的

🎧 Track 126

中式英文 Setting up a professional stand is good to lift up our image.

老外這樣說 **Setting up a professional-looking booth will help us raise our profile.**

 大師提點

"Stand" 的意思比較接近「小攤子」，比方說 "fruit stand"（水果攤），因此用 professional 來形容，語意有點奇怪。若是使用 "a professional-looking booth" 即可表達「顯得很專業的參展攤位」了。另外，要表示「提升形象」，動詞部分不能使用 "lift up" 這個片語，因其涵義為「吊起／舉起」，並不適合用在此情境。

 實境對話

A: **Why are we spending so much on the booth?**
B: **Setting up a professional-looking booth will help us raise our profile.**
　A：為什麼我們要花這麼多錢在攤位上？
　B：設置一個專業的攤位有助於提升我們的形象。

📢 **老外還會這樣說**

❏ **We need a professional booth to make a good impression.**
　我們需要一個專業的攤位來創造良好的印象。

❏ **We can save a little money by going with a standard design.**
　如果採用標準風格的設計，我們就能省下一些錢。

Unit 10

🔍 **關鍵字**

booth [buθ] (*n.*) 攤位；隔間
profile [ˋprofaɪl] (*n.*) 側影；形象；人物簡介
impression [ɪmˋprɛʃən] (*n.*) 印象
standard [ˋstændəd] (*adj.*) 標準的

中式英文　Hello. Welcome to visit us.

老外這樣說　**Hello. Please come in and have a look around.**

 大師提點

此句要點是邀請客戶進到攤位來「參觀」。說成 "visit us" 是不對的，因為 "visit" 是「拜訪／探視」的意思。若說成 "Please come in and have a look around."，聽起來就自然許多。

實境對話

A: **Hello. Please come in and have a look around.**
B: **Nice to meet you.**
　A：您好，歡迎光臨，請隨意看看。
　B：你好。

 老外還會這樣說

❏ Hello. I'm Darren Lee, Director of Product Development at Everclever.
您好，我是 Everclever 產品開發部的主管李岱倫。

❏ I'd love to sit down with you and discuss our products.
我很希望能和您坐下來聊聊我們的產品。

❏ We've got some great new products. Let me show you.
本公司有許多非常棒的新產品。讓我為您做個介紹。

❏ So, what brings you to the expo?
那，您來參觀這次展覽的目的是什麼？

🔍 **關鍵字**

director [dəˋrɛktə] (n.) 主管；董事
expo = exposition 展覽

歡迎來看看我們的樣品。這本是我們的最新產品型錄。

Track 128

中式英文　Welcome to take a look at our samples. This is the catalog of our latest products.

老外這樣說　**Feel free to have a look at our demonstration models. And this is our latest brochure.**

 大師提點

在展場站攤位時要吸引客戶前來參觀，"Welcome to take a look at …." 聽起來不如 "Feel free to look at …." 來得親切。此外，"demonstration model" 比 "sample" 更可顯示出動態展示的感覺。

 實境對話

A: Feel free to have a look at our demonstration models. And this is our latest brochure.
B: OK, thanks.
　A：歡迎參考我們展示的型號。這是本公司最新的宣傳冊。
　B：好的，謝謝。

🧑‍🦯 老外還會這樣說

❏ Would you like to try a sample?
您想要試試樣品嗎？

❏ Go ahead and take a sample with you.
歡迎索取樣品。

❏ Would you like a brochure?
您需要一份宣傳冊嗎？

❏ Here's my card. You can download a catalog from our website.
這是我的名片。您可以從我們的網站上下載型錄。

Unit 10

🔍 關鍵字

latest [`letɪst] (adj.) 最新的
sample [`sæmpl] (n.) 樣品

brochure [bro`ʃʊr] (n.) 小冊子
catalog [`kætəlɔg] (n.) 型錄

有興趣參加我們的比賽嗎？有機會贏得免費的 iPad 喔！

 Track 129

中式英文 Are you interested in participating in our competition? You may win a free iPad.

老外這樣說 **Are you interested in entering our contest for a free iPad?**

大師提點

邀請民眾參加活動，使用 "participate in our competition" 會給人像是要參與激烈競賽的感覺，但通常展場所舉辦的「比賽」大多是小遊戲，例如有獎問答等，因此，用 "enter our contest" 表達即可。

實境對話

A: Hello! Are you interested in entering our contest for a free iPad?
B: No, thanks.

A：您好！有沒有興趣參加我們的比賽？有機會贏得一台 iPad 喔。
B：不用了，謝謝。

老外還會這樣說

❏ **Would you like to enter a drawing for a free iPad?**
您要不要參加能免費獲得 iPad 的抽獎活動？

❏ **Everything in the booth is 20% off until the end of the day today.**
今天之內，攤位上的所有商品都打八折。

關鍵字

contest [kən`tɛst] (n.) 比賽　　　　　**drawing** [`drɔɪŋ] (n.) 抽獎

⚠ 職場成功 Tips

要邀請潛在客戶到攤位上參觀，利用競賽或小活動是方式之一。另可依照公司屬性，先想好 "conversation opener"（對話開場白）來吸引目光，比方說："Did you get your free ...?"（您拿到免費的……贈品了嗎？）等。

我很樂意為您示範產品操作。

中式英文 | I'm glad to operate the product for you.

老外這樣說 | **I'd be happy to give you a demonstration.**

 大師提點

此句要點是「做示範／實際操作產品」給客戶看，不可直譯為 "operate the product"（操作產品），英文並無此說法。應直接用 "demonstration"（示範）一字來表達。

 實境對話

A: How does it work exactly?
B: I'd be happy to give you a demonstration.

　A：它到底該怎麼操作？
　B：我很樂意為您做個示範。

📣 **老外還會這樣說**

❏ **Let me show you how it works.**
讓我為您示範它的操作方式。

❏ **You'll be surprised what this can do.**
您一定想不到它有什麼樣的功能。

❏ **Have you used one of these before?**
您曾經使用過這類的產品嗎？

❏ **Go ahead and try it.**
歡迎試用。

Unit
10

🔍 **關鍵字**

demonstration [ˌdɛmən`streʃən] (n.) 示範

您可以隨時打我們的免付費專線訂貨。

Track 131

中式英文 You may call this number without charge to place an order anytime.

老外這樣說 **You can place an order anytime by calling our toll-free number.**

大師提點

展場中現場馬上下訂單的機會較少，通常客戶會在評估之後才決定。一般「下訂單」就說 "place an order"；「免付費電話」若說成 "a number without charge" 老外有可能聽不懂！正確的說法應為 "a toll-free number"。

實境對話

A: Thanks for your time. I'll think about it.
B: You're welcome. You can place an order anytime by calling our toll-free number.

　A：謝謝你花時間為我介紹。我考慮一下。
　B：不客氣。您隨時可以撥打我們的免付費電話訂貨。

老外還會這樣說

❏ Remember, the 15% discount is only available if you place your order before 6:30 tonight.
請記住，您必須在今天晚上六點半之前下訂，才能獲得八五折的優惠。

❏ Do you have a business card? I'd be happy to let you know about any special offers that come along.
您有名片嗎？只要有任何特別優惠時，我很樂意通知您一聲。

❏ If you order through our website, enter the offer code E-X-P-O to get free shipping.
如果您要從我們的網站下訂，請輸入優惠碼 E-X-P-O，您的商品就能免運費。

🔍 關鍵字

toll-free number 免付費電話　　　　**offer code** 優惠碼

這款非常暢銷，而且目前正在促銷。

中式英文 This one is hot goods, and now we're providing a promotion.

老外這樣說 **This one is our best seller, and we're currently offering a discount on it.**

 大師提點

每家公司都有其賣得最好的產品，但若將「熱賣商品」直譯為 "hot goods" 那可就不妙了，因為英文裡的 "hot goods" 是指「贓物」！此處使用 "best seller" 這個片語才不至於產生誤會。另外，雖然 "promotion" 是促銷的意思，但是在國外通常會直接表示「提供折扣」，因此只要說 "offer a discount" 即可。

 實境對話

A: **This one is our best seller, and we're currently offering a discount on it.**

B: **That's good to know.**

A：這是我們銷售最好的產品，本公司目前正針對它提供優惠。

B：那真是好消息。

🔊 **老外還會這樣說**

❏ **This is our top-of-the-line model.**
這是本公司最頂級的型號。

❏ **We offer a five-year warranty—by far the longest in the industry.**
本公司提供五年保固，這是目前為止業界最長的保固年限。

🔍 **關鍵字**

top-of-the-line（同類商品中）最頂級的　　**warranty** [ˋwɔrəntɪ] (n.) 保固

⚠ **職場成功 Tips**

在展場中為吸引潛在客戶，強調優惠價格是方法之一，不過亦可突顯「老外還會這樣說」例句中提到的 "quality"（品質）、"warranty"（保固）等其他 unique selling proposition (USP)——產品賣點。

🔊 Track 133

中式英文　Our parts are almost from Japan.

老外這樣說　**We source most of the components from Japan.**

 大師提點

"Our parts are almost from Japan." 應該是大部分人第一時間會想到的說法，雖然沒有錯，但是專業度略顯不足。換個說法，我們可以 "source" 這個字來表示「由 [某來源] 獲得 [某物]」。另外，使用較專業的 "components" 一字取代 "parts"，同樣表達「機器設備的構成零件」之意。

 實境對話

A: Is this made locally?

B: We source most of the components from Japan.

　A：這是在本地製作的嗎？

　B：我們大部分的零件都是從日本進口的。

📣 **老外還會這樣說**

❏ **Yes. Designed and built right here in Taiwan.**

是的，全都是在台灣設計、製造的。

❏ **The chips are Korean, but the rest was made and assembled locally.**

晶片是從韓國來的，但是剩下的全都是在本地製造與組裝的。

❏ **It's actually manufactured in Italy. We're the official sales representative in Taiwan.**

它其實是在義大利製造的。我們是台灣的官方銷售代表商。

🔍 **關鍵字**

component [kəm`ponənt] (n.) 零件

chip [tʃɪp] (n.) 晶片

assemble [ə`sɛmbl] (v.) 組裝

official [ə`fɪʃəl] (adj.) 官方的；正式的

產品的報價會依您的訂購數量有所不同。

🎵 **Track 134**

中式英文 The quotation of our products will depend on the quantity.

老外這樣說 **It depends on the size of the order. Let me give you a quote.**

⚡ 大師提點

因為中英文的句子結構不同,一句中文在英文裡可能要分兩句講;有時兩句中文的意思用英文表達只需一句話。中式英文例句的文法沒錯,不過老外通常不會這麼說。另外,"quotation" 指「報價單」,一般而言是書面用語,用在口語表達就太文謅謅了。

實境對話

A: How much do these cost?
B: It depends on the size of the order. Let me give you a quote.

A:這些東西需要多少錢?
B:價格取決於訂單的大小。我先幫您估個價。

📢 老外還會這樣說

❑ **How many were you thinking of purchasing?**
您考慮購買幾個?

❑ **How many units are we talking about?**
您打算要買幾組?

❑ **I'd be happy to provide you with a quote.**
我很樂意為您提供報價。

❑ **Let's sit down and I'll show you how our pricing works.**
我們先坐下來,讓我向您解釋本公司的計價方式。

Unit
10

🔍 關鍵字

quote [kwot] (*n.*) 報價
quotation [kwoˋteʃən] (*n.*) 報價單

Unit 11

★ ★ ★ ★ ★ ★ ★ ★ ★ ★ ★ ★ ★ ★ ★ ★ ★ ★ ★ ★

出差旅遊

Traveling

你可以告訴我登機門在哪個方向嗎？

🎵 Track 135

中式英文 ┃ Could you tell me the boarding gate is in which direction?

老外這樣說 **Could you point me toward the gate?**

💡 大師提點

在機場難免會有跟人家問路的時候，但若像中式英文 "Can you tell me … in which direction?" 完全是中文的直譯，英文並不會這樣說。此處只要精簡地說 "Could you point me toward [place]?"，就能傳達「麻煩你幫我指出 [某處] 的方向」的意思。

實境對話

A: You'll have to hurry to catch your flight, sir.

B: OK. Could you point me toward the gate?

A：先生，您如果想搭上飛機，就必須快一點了。

B：好的。你能不能告訴我登機門在哪個方向？

老外還會這樣説

❏ **Could you tell me where Gate 104 is?**

你能不能告訴我 104 號登機門在哪裡？

❏ **Excuse me, how do I get to Gate 211 from here?**

不好意思，從這裡要怎麼到 211 號登機門？

❏ **Is this the way to the International Terminal?**

到國際航廈是走這邊嗎？

🔍 關鍵字

terminal [ˋtɝmən]] (n.) 航空站

⚠ 職場成功 Tips

除了上述 "Could you point me toward [place]?" 句型之外，問路時常用的句型還包括：

- Could you please tell me where [place] is?（你可以跟我說 [某處] 在哪裡嗎？）
- Please tell me how I can get to [somewhere].（請告訴我怎麼到 [某地]。）
- Where is [somewhere]?（[某地] 在哪裡？）

我可以在這裡兌現旅行支票嗎？

中式英文　Can I exchange my traveler's check to cash here?

老外這樣說　**Can I cash my traveler's checks here?**

💡 大師提點

「兌現旅行支票」怎麼說？英文並沒有 "exchange my traveler's check to cash" 這種說法。正確的表達方式是 "cash my traveler's check"。

實境對話

A: **Can I cash my traveler's checks here?**

B: **You can use them at a hotel, but to cash them you should go to a bank.**

　A：我能不能在這裡兌現旅行支票？

　B：你可以在飯店直接使用旅行支票，不過如果你要換現金的話，就應該去銀行。

老外還會這樣說

❏ **There's an ATM machine in the shopping arcade.**

購物中心裡有一台提款機。

❏ **Yes, we can cash them for you, but there's a 5% service charge.**

可以，我們能為您兌換現金，但是會收取百分之五的手續費。

❏ **I'm sorry, we stopped accepting traveler's checks last year.**

很抱歉，我們從去年開始就不接受旅行支票了。

❏ **I'm sorry, we only accept cash or credit.**

很抱歉，我們只收現金或信用卡。

Unit
11

🔍 關鍵字

traveler's check 旅行支票

arcade [ɑr`ked] (n.) 長廊商場

service charge 手續費

我們遇到幾個大亂流，全程大家都嚇壞了。

| 中式英文 | We met some big turbulence, and we were afraid of them all the way. |

| 老外這樣說 | **We ran into some severe turbulence. We were scared the whole time.** |

💡 大師提點

此句包含三個重點。首先，「遇到」不能直譯為 "meet"（遇見／會面），使用片語 "run into" 可帶出「偶遇／碰上」之意。接著，「大亂流」中所指的「大」在此情境以 "severe"（劇烈的／嚴重的）一字較為貼切。最後，"be afraid" 是「害怕」的意思，和「被嚇到」是不一樣的，因此用 "be scared" 來傳達語意才正確。

實境對話

A: **How was your flight?**
B: **We ran into some severe turbulence. We were scared the whole time.**

A：你的飛行旅途如何？
B：我們遇到了幾個嚴重的亂流，整個航程大家都感到很驚恐。

老外還會這樣說

❏ **Don't ask. The turbulence was so bad the seatbelt sign was on for the whole flight.**
別提了。亂流嚴重到安全帶警示燈全程都是亮著的。

❏ **Great. We practically had the whole plane to ourselves.**
非常好。整架飛機幾乎沒什麼其他乘客。

🔍 關鍵字

turbulence [ˋtɝbjələns] (n.) 亂流　　**practically** [ˋpræktɪklɪ] (adv.) 幾乎；差不多

⚠️ 職場成功 Tips

筆者聽過很多同學將「我不怕熱」直譯為 "I'm not afraid of hot weather."，但老外並不會這麼說，因為「怕熱」的「怕」並不是指「害怕」。因此，這句話用英文應說成 "Hot weather doesn't bother me that much."（炎熱天氣對我並不會造成困擾。）

這筆款項我要刷卡。

中式英文　Please charge the money on my credit card.

老外這樣說　**Just put it on my card, please.**

 大師提點

動詞 "charge" 的確指「收取費用」，但是「款項」不能直譯成 "money"（錢財）。這句話很常用也很簡單，只要說 "put the amount on my card" 就可以傳達「將金額記到信用卡的帳上」之意了。

實境對話

A: **How would you like to pay the bill?**

B: **Just put it on my card, please.**

　A：您想要如何付帳呢？

　B：請從我的信用卡扣款。

 老外還會這樣說

❏ **Do you accept JCB?**

你們接受 JCB 卡嗎？

❏ **Could you charge everything to my company account?**

你可不可以把所有款項記在我公司的帳戶上？

❏ **Could I arrange a direct bank transfer?**

我可以直接轉帳嗎？

❏ **I'd like to use traveler's checks, if that's OK.**

如果可以的話，我想用旅行支票。

Unit 11

關鍵字

accept [ək`sɛpt] (v.) 接受

charge [tʃɑrdʒ] (v.) 收費；記帳

我想要一張本市的地圖，謝謝。對了，你們有公車時刻表嗎？

🎧 Track 139

中式英文
I want a map of this city, thank you. And do you have a bus timetable?

老外這樣說
I'd like a map of the city, please. Oh, and do you have a bus schedule by any chance?

💡 大師提點

跟人要求東西，使用 "I'd like a [something], please." 這個句型比較有禮貌。另外，在美國，「公車時刻表」較常用的說法為 "bus schedule"。除此之外，"by chance"（恰巧地）也是本句重點之一，雖然在中譯裡未必會被逐字翻出，但是此片語讓整句話傳達出言下之意：「你們若剛好有公車時刻表，請給我一份。」

實境對話

A: Welcome to the visitor's center. What can I do for you?
B: I'd like a map of the city, please. Oh, and do you have a bus schedule by any chance?

A：歡迎來到遊客中心。我能為您做什麼嗎？
B：請給我一張本市的地圖。噢，對了，你們這裡有沒有公車時刻表？

老外還會這樣說

❏ **Do you have any information on local city tours?**
你們有市內觀光的行程資訊嗎？

❏ **Do you have a list of recommended restaurants?**
你們有沒有推薦的餐廳名單？

❏ **We're looking for somewhere fun to go tonight. Any ideas?**
我們在找今晚可以去玩的地方。有任何點子嗎？

🔍 關鍵字

by chance 碰巧；偶然地

真抱歉我們遲到了。附近的停車位有點難找。

中式英文 So sorry we're late. It's hard to find a parking space here.

老外這樣說 **I'm so sorry we're late. We had trouble parking.**

💡 大師提點

中式英文例句 "It's hard to ..." 用了虛主詞 "it"，略嫌「拐彎抹角」，不如使用 "We/I have trouble/problem/difficulty + Ving." 句型，直接傳達「某人做某事有困難」之意比較符合老外說話的習慣。

實境對話

A: Ms. Chen. I'm glad you made it.

B: I'm so sorry we're late. We had trouble parking.

　A：陳小姐，真高興妳到了。

　B：真抱歉我們遲到了。我們找不到停車位。

老外還會這樣說

❑ **Sorry we're late. We had a little trouble finding the place.**
對不起，我們遲到了。我們找了一陣子才找到這個地方。

❑ **Sorry we're late. We had a little car trouble.**
抱歉，我們遲到了。我們的車子出了點狀況。

🔍 關鍵字

make it 成功；趕到

⚠ 職場成功 Tips

路上的交通狀況難以預料，以下皆可用來說明遇到「塞車」：

- There was a big traffic jam.
- There was a lot of traffic.
- It was bumper to bumper all the way here.

Track 141

中式英文 Is it easy to get here?

老外這樣說 **Did you have any trouble finding the place?**

大師提點

承上題，相反地「路 / 地方好找嗎？」用 "Do you have trouble + Ving ...?" 此句型來表達也是比較道地的說法。的確，老外平常在說的英文及他們描述事情的思維和中文有相當大的差異，多練習幾次就能習慣成「自然」！

實境對話

A: **Did you have any trouble finding the place?**
B: **Not at all. Your directions were very clear.**

　A：這個地方會不會很難找？
　B：一點也不會，你的指示非常清楚。

老外還會這樣説

❏ **Hi, Paula. It's so good to see you.**
嗨，寶拉。真高興見到妳。

❏ **Hi, Paula. Come on in.**
嗨，寶拉。快進來吧！

❏ **Hi, Paula. Can I help you with your bag?**
嗨，寶拉。我幫妳提袋子好嗎？

❏ **Hi, Paula. Let me take your coat for you.**
嗨，寶拉。我幫妳把外套掛起來。

關鍵字

direction [dəˋrɛkʃən] (n.) 方向；指示

我的班機誤點，所以我錯過轉機了。

🎧 Track **142**

中式英文　My flight's arrival was delayed, so I missed the transfer.

老外這樣說　**My flight got in late so I missed my connection.**

💡 大師提點

首先，「我的班機誤點」該如何表達？ "My flight's arrival was delayed" 顯然是中式英文，通常老外並不會這樣說。不用想得太複雜，直接說 "My flight got in late" 就可以了。另外，"transfer" 一字是指車輛的轉乘，而「轉機」的英文是 "connection"（接駁轉運的航班）。

實境對話

A: Where are you now?
B: I'm still in Chicago. My flight got in late so I missed my connection.

A：你現在在哪裡？
B：我還在芝加哥。因為班機誤點，所以我沒搭上轉機的航班。

老外還會這樣說

❏ **I'm still in Tokyo. My flight was cancelled.**
我還在東京。我的班機被取消掉了。

❏ **I'm in Paris. My connecting flight was delayed.**
我在巴黎。我要轉乘的班機誤點了。

❏ **I'm still in Sydney. There was a mechanical problem with the plane.**
我人還在雪梨。飛機出了點機械問題。

❏ **I'm stuck in Denver. There's a blizzard and they closed the airport.**
我被困在丹佛。機場因為暴風雪而關閉了。

Unit
11

🔍 關鍵字

mechanical [mə`kænɪkḷ] (adj.) 機械的
blizzard [`blɪzəd] (n.) 暴風雪

請問怎麼去火車站最快？

中式英文 How to go to the train station most quickly?

老外這樣說 **Could you tell me the quickest way to get to the train station from here?**

⚡ 大師提點

此句要點為以最快的方式到達某地的說法。提到「最快」，許多人只想到 "most quickly"，但老外通常會用 "the quickest way" 來表達。

 實境對話

A: Excuse me. Could you tell me the quickest way to get to the train station from here?

B: It's a little far to walk. Why don't you take a cab?

A：不好意思，你能不能告訴我從這裡到火車站最快的方式？

B：走路有點遠。你何不搭計程車？

 老外還會這樣說

❏ **Is a taxi the best way to get to the train station?**

搭計程車是去火車站最好的方法嗎？

❏ **Where can I catch a cab?**

我要到哪裡搭計程車？

❏ **Can I get to the train station by bus?**

我可以搭公車到火車站嗎？

❏ **Is there a subway station around here?**

這附近有沒有地鐵站？

🔍 關鍵字

cab [kæb] (n.) 計程車

⚠ 職場成功 Tips

大部分的交通工具相信讀者們都已經很熟悉，而台北市相當便利的 "YouBike" 系統，其正式英文名稱叫做 "bike sharing system"。

在我們去辦公室之前，您想吃點東西嗎？

中式英文 Do you want to eat something before we go to the office?

老外這樣說 **Do you want to stop and get something to eat on the way to the office?**

大師提點

如何用英文口語表達「隨便吃點東西」？其實根本不需要什麼太高深的字彙，只要說 "get something to eat" 即可。另外還有一個重點，既然是隨便吃，就不會是坐在餐廳好好地享用，因此在句尾加一個片語 "on the way to [somewhere]"（在前往 [某處] 途中）則顯得更加自然。

實境對話

A: Do you want to stop and get something to eat on the way to the office?

B: I'm OK, thanks. Go ahead and get something for yourself if you want, though.

A：你想要在前往辦公室的途中吃點東西嗎？

B：不用了，謝謝。不過如果你想吃點什麼的話，就去買吧。

老外還會這樣說

❏ Is there anything I can get for you before we go?
在我們出發之前，需要我幫你弄點什麼嗎？

❏ Are you all ready to go?
你們都準備好出發了嗎？

❏ Did you bring a coat? It's pretty cold outside.
你有沒有帶外套？外面還蠻冷的。

❏ It'll take us about an hour to get downtown.
我們大概要花一小時才能抵達市中心。

Unit 11

關鍵字

downtown [ˌdaʊnˋtaʊn] (n.) 市中心

Track 145

中式英文 Welcome to Taipei office. Hope you like here.

老外這樣說 **Welcome to the Taipei office. We hope you enjoy your time here with us.**

 大師提點

此句重點在於「希望你會喜歡此地」的道地口語。"Hope you like here." 並不符合文法，因為 here 是副詞，如果一定要說應改成 "Hope you like it here."。不過相較之下，老外常說的 "enjoy your time here" 更能傳達希望「你在此處的這段時間內，所經歷的事情你都會喜歡」的親切感。

 實境對話

A: Welcome to the Taipei office, Mr. Bryant. We hope you enjoy your time here with us.

B: Thank you. I'm looking forward to working with all of you.

A：布萊恩先生，歡迎來到台北辦公室。希望您在我們這兒一切順心。

B：謝謝你。我一直都很期待和各位一起工作。

老外還會這樣說

❑ Mr. Bryant. Welcome to Taipei. I'm Vivian Chou.
布萊恩先生，歡迎來到台北。我是周薇安。

❑ I'll be your main contact person while you're in town.
在您到訪的這段期間，我將是您的主要聯繫人員。

❑ If there's anything I can do for you while you're here, don't hesitate to ask.
如果您在這兒的這段期間內有任何我可以協助您的事情，請不用客氣，隨時告訴我。

❑ Please let me know if there's anything I can do to make your stay more comfortable.
如果有任何我份內能使您這趟行程更加舒適的需求，請和我說一聲。

關鍵字

hesitate [ˋhɛzəˌtet] (v.) 猶豫；遲疑

Track 146

中式英文 The England people are very friendly. I want to go there again right away.

老外這樣說 **People in England are amazingly friendly. I can't wait to go back.**

大師提點

要表達「英國人」有以下幾種說法："people in England"、"English people" 或 "the British" 等。此外，「想馬上……」在口語中有一個實用性相當高的句型可運用，也就是 "I can't wait to + V."（我等不及做某事了。）聽起來比起直譯的句子更生動。

 實境對話

A: How was your trip?
B: Great. People in England are amazingly friendly. I can't wait to go back.
　A：你的旅程如何？
　B：很棒。英國人非常地友善。我等不及再去一次。

 老外還會這樣說

❏ **Awesome. Everyone in the San Francisco office was really helpful. You'll get along really well with them.**
超棒的！舊金山分部的每個人都非常熱心幫忙，你一定能和他們打成一片。

❏ **Not bad. I had some good meetings, but I couldn't get used to the food.**
還不錯。幾場會議都很順利，不過那裡的食物我吃不慣。

❏ **Terrible. The deal didn't go through and it rained the whole time.**
糟透了。不但案子沒談成，整趟旅程還都在下雨。

Unit
11

關鍵字

amazingly [ə`mezɪŋlɪ] (*adv.*) 令人驚訝地
get used to 習慣

awesome [`ɔsəm] (*adj.*) 棒透了的
deal [dil] (*n.*) 交易

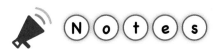

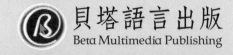

國家圖書館出版品預行編目資料

外商・百大英文口語勝經 / 薛詠文作. -- 初版. -- 臺北市
：貝塔, 2013.11
面； 公分
ISBN 978-957-729-940-6（平裝附光碟片）
1.商業英文 2.會話
805.188 102020412

外商・百大英文口語勝經
145 Essential Phrases for Business Conversation

作　　者 / 薛詠文
英文審定 / David Katz
執行編輯 / 游玉旻

出　　版 / 貝塔出版有限公司
地　　址 / 100 台北市中正區館前路 12 號 11 樓
電　　話 / (02) 2314-2525
傳　　真 / (02) 2312-3535
郵　　撥 / 19493777 貝塔出版有限公司
客服專線 / (02) 2314-3535
客服信箱 / btservice@betamedia.com.tw

經　　銷 / 時報文化出版企業股份有限公司
地　　址 / 桃園市龜山區萬壽路二段 351 號
電　　話 / 02-2306-6842

出版日期 / 2017 年 8 月初版四刷
定　　價 / 280 元
Ｉ Ｓ Ｂ Ｎ / 978-957-729-940-6

喚醒你的英文語感！

對折後釘好，直接寄回即可！

廣 告 回 信
北區郵政管理局登記證
北 台 字 第 1 4 2 5 6 號
免 貼 郵 票

100 台北市中正區館前路12號11樓

 貝塔語言出版 收
Beta Multimedia Publishing

寄件者住址 □□□

謝謝您購買本書！！

貝塔語言擁有最優良之英文學習書籍，為提供您最佳的英語學習資訊，您可填妥此表後寄回（免貼郵票）將可不定期收到本公司最新發行書訊及活動訊息！

姓名：_____　性別：□男 □女　生日：_____年_____月_____日

電話：(公)_____(宅)_____(手機)_____

電子信箱：_____

學歷：□高中職含以下　□專科　□大學　□研究所含以上

職業：□金融　□服務　□傳播　□製造　□資訊　□軍公教　□出版

　　　□自由　□教育　□學生　□其他

職級：□企業負責人　□高階主管　□中階主管　□職員　□專業人士

1.您購買的書籍是？_____

2.您從何處得知本產品？(可複選)

　　　□書店 □網路 □書展 □校園活動 □廣告信函 □他人推薦 □新聞報導 □其他

3.您覺得本產品價格：

　　　□偏高 □合理 □偏低

4.請問目前您每週花了多少時間學英語？

　　　□ 不到十分鐘 □ 十分鐘以上，但不到半小時 □ 半小時以上，但不到一小時

　　　□ 一小時以上，但不到兩小時 □ 兩個小時以上 □ 不一定

5.通常在選擇語言學習書時，哪些因素是您會考慮的？

　　　□ 封面 □ 內容、實用性 □ 品牌 □ 媒體、朋友推薦 □ 價格□ 其他_____

6.市面上您最需要的語言書種類為？

　　　□ 聽力 □ 閱讀 □ 文法 □ 口說 □ 寫作 □ 其他_____

7.通常您會透過何種方式選購語言學習書籍？

　　　□ 書店門市 □ 網路書店 □ 郵購 □ 直接找出版社 □ 學校或公司團購

　　　□ 其他_____

8.給我們的建議：_____

_____

喚醒你的英文語感！

Get a Feel for English !

喚醒你的英文語感！

Get a Feel for English !